Christian Bedor
The Confession

Christian Bedor
The Confession
Fictitious autobiography
of a Catholic main teacher's son

Bibliographic Information of the German Library
The German Library lists this publication in the
German national bibliography; detailed bibliographic data
can be found on the Internet at http://dnb.ddb.de

müll-zeit-lose™ and Personalberatung Team Verreckt™
www.muell-zeit-lose.de

Translated from German into English by Valerie Smith
© 2019 Bedor, Christian
Production and publishing: BoD – Books on Demand,
Norderstedt
ISBN: 9783746009476

For Ewa

Table of contents

Early days 9
Scooter 14
My brother 18
Flashlight 21
Vormstein 23
Pumpkin 33
Mark 38
Capri ice cream 41
The Confession 51
First Holy Communion 60
The new priest 68
The forbidden tree 75
Bärbel 77
The new village school 84
Hahn 90
The Gymnasium 93
The small official residence 100
To Dortmund 105
Ministrant with Uncle Eberhard 108
Curriculum Vitae 119
Publications 120

It was Good Friday, 7:15 p.m. in the apartment. My 36-year-old mother was lying on the living room couch when I was born in the late 1950s on the first floor of the rubble stone village school in Kleinenbach. The only village doctor and the midwife helped. At the same time my father, who was two years older, played the organ in the church, which was only a stone's throw away. He practiced for the Easter masses.

After the rehearsal he came home and assumed that I had not yet been born, because the bedding was put on just as it was in the afternoon when he left us.

"When will the child come?" he asked.

"Thomas is back there," my mother replied.

I was lying in a cot in her bedroom. I had four fingers of my left hand in my mouth and sucked on them. It was dark. Noises penetrated my auricles. But that didn't bother me.

My mother never gave me the breast. My 5-year-old sister Marlene was the last one to enjoy it. Unfortunately she chewed the nipples so much that I was denied this tenderness forever.

I can't remember a baby photo, but I can remember the fact that my 7-year-old brother Clemens was a supporter of another little brother before I was born - as he later told me. He therefore engaged in a pillow fight in the nursery with my two sisters who wanted a girl. At the baptism I had contact with Father Seedorn for the first time, but he did not remain in my memory for the following years.

The time without school went by without any incidents. Except for teething troubles. My one year younger friend Peter asked me one afternoon not to get too close to him. Which I then avoided. We stood about six meters opposite each other and the following day I lay in bed with chicken-pox.

Peter was the son of the cleaning woman of the school. He mostly wore knee breeches made of light brown leather. And a sweater. Summer shorts. With a shirt. Mostly robust closed low shoes, which were laced at the sides. Peter had a round face, a fine physiognomy. He was good and had nothing slit-origin - just like me. However, he wore a hedgehog haircut. We liked to play together.

In the early afternoon the sky was overcast, a little cloudy. As it sometimes is to the end of winter. I played alone at a puddle in front of the school, pulled connecting channels with the rubber boot heel to the next-smaller pond, thought of Peter and watched the slowly flowing water daydreaming. I was busy. Only good thing it had rained before. My mother had told me in the morning not to leave the house because doctors and other people were coming. It's about school enrollment. My mother didn't make much of a fuss about such examinations or about the appointment. I was briefly and succinctly reminded of this.

I was surprised that no other child was playing in the puddles. I would have loved company so much. My 15-year-old sister Veronika always got up early to take a bus to the nun's school. My other two siblings were now in class.

Peter didn't have time because his father had died. He had been a lumberjack. He was rarely seen in the village. I only saw him sometimes when I visited Peter on the village slope. Mühlenhofs had their own house. Newly built. With balcony. And white house walls. Everything smelled new in it and it formed the final house in a cul-de-sac that led up the mountain. There was a small turning area for cars. The house could be reached on foot via a narrow stairway on the steep slope.

I played in the puddles and looked at the circles that were now formed by raindrops on the surface of the water. Peter's mother had told my mother that her husband had been laid out in the house for a while. A neighbor was on wake duty at the time. When a storm came, she shouted, "Woman, woman, he's blue!"

I was frightened that Peter's father had died because I always thought fathers with young children could not die. I kept thinking they couldn't die until their children were grown.

Besides, I'd never seen a corpse before. I couldn't figure out why a dead man would turn blue in a thunderstorm. Did that also apply to the dead in the graves? The performance scared me very much and I avoided the contact with Peter for several days.

My mother appeared at the window and called me to her house. It was time and I should come, especially since I had to wash and change.

I regretted this, then looked back at my puddle, put both hands in my pockets and went to school. In the bathroom I took off my clothes, washed myself and got fresh clothes from my mother.

Then we entered a classroom on the ground floor, which was now furnished as an examination room. Most of the chairs and tables were on the walls.

Except for a few adults in white coats, there were a lot of kids here with their mothers. Some fathers among them. Some children I knew by sight, but many were unknown to me. That wasn't surprising, because I didn't attend a kindergarten where I could have found more friends. My parents thought the church kindergarten was unsuitable. Because of the nuns.

"Thomas Lehr, please come here," called a nurse standing next to a doctor.

The examination was carried out quickly. Measure, weigh, grasp with the right arm over the head and touch the left auricle with the fingers. The teeth were examined, the left upper arm was scratched. Then my mother helped me get dressed.

The first day of school wasn't exciting. There wasn't a school bag for me. My parents didn't think it was necessary. Some kids had school cones. I don't remember a school photo.

Our class consisted of two vintages. In front sat the I-males and behind them the former I-males. Our teacher's name was Grewen. She was slender, brunette, with a slight silver glance. I fell in love with her after a while. The young Catholic teacher had to teach both classes at the same time. It was her first teaching position after her legal clerkship. Miss Grewen was about 23 years old.

Restlessness often arose in the classroom, but with her austere gaze she immediately stopped it. I found it annoying to sit in this class with the older know-alls on my back. That's why I didn't check in. I felt uncomfortable because it seemed to me that the second graders knew every answer to questions to the first class. That thought intimidated me.

One day I enjoyed sleeping longer and playing with my matchbox cars. My mother was there and wondered at first that I had so much time in the morning.

Around ten o'clock I entered the empty classroom and saw notebooks and pencils on the tables. The knapsacks were next to the benches. My classmates had to be here early. I went outside.

"Are you sick?" asked my classmate Tobias, whom I met first in the schoolyard during the break. He was the son of a better-off family and very hard-boiled. He didn't mind lying or stealing chewing gum.

So in passing.

Tobias was petite, narrow-faced. I was impressed how he moved like a cat in sports. So from now on he was my best friend and I preferred to play with him rather than with Peter.

"No, I'm not sick!" I replied.

"Why do you ask...?"

"We've been here since 7:30!"

I got queasy. I had never been late and had thought that classes would start at ten today. What would Miss Grewen do?

With my knees trembling, I entered the classroom. As soon as it was quiet in the room, she confronted me. I didn't know how to answer their questions. What was I supposed to say? That I was wrong? That's what I didn't feel ashamed of.

"You'll be in the afternoon this afternoon," she said. "Two hours."

My heart pounded in my throat.

I didn't expect such a drastic punishment. What would my mother, who used to be a teacher, say? And my father first?

It is horrible to be publicly punished so exposed and not to be able to defend oneself out of powerlessness and guilt. My friend Tobias would have thought of a plausible explanation at that moment. Probably would have lied and been off the hook. Maybe he would have said something about abdominal pain. Or a squirrel that was rushing around the living room and he should have caught it. His family and he lived in their own large house on the edge of the forest. It wouldn't have been unusual if a curious squirrel had gotten lost on the balcony. Whether it's a lie or a truth. No one could check it out. Tobias wouldn't have taken his breath away. He would have known a way out and got away blameless.

So after I had confessed the misfortune to my mother at lunch, and she was very angry about it, I sat in a girl's class. It was a higher class who had manual work lessons with Miss Grewen in the afternoon. Crochet, knit, sew. I was

13

sitting in the back of the room, getting math assignments and torturing myself with them. At that time I swore to myself never to forget the lesson times again.

What a humiliation. The assignments were exhausting. But the girls with their knitting were kind to me. It was a welcome change for her to have a boy from one of the lower classes with her. They were amazed at my presence and a girl asked me quietly why I had to detain.

When Miss Grewen turned to some students in the front row of the bench to show them more of the art of knitting, another girl sitting near me helped me find a solution. That was a punishable offense. I was very scared. Probably I would get another punishment - and so would the helper! How was I supposed to make that clear to the girl?

But luckily, we weren't caught.

Scooter

On this sunny summer afternoon our Llyod 400 parked parallel to the stone flight of steps. He even had a folding sunroof. He was dark blue and parked so that an adult could walk between him and the stairs. My father, the only one in the family who had a driver's license, apparently had to leave again. Otherwise he would have put the car in the converted pigsty.

With the scooter, which belonged to my brother Clemens, had inflatable tires and no solid rubber tires, I drove back and forth in front of the stairs and the tree row.

Sometimes I would wiggle between the trees or drive behind the building where the schoolyard was fenced. Here there was a large sawdust box which was used in sports lessons so that schoolchildren could learn to jump. When there were no lessons, sometimes small children played in

14

this box. Occasionally, older people also came and played batting ball.

Then the sawdust box was her mark.

No one was on the square that afternoon. In short trousers and a summer shirt I drove over it, lost in thought, and headed back to school to see if my father had come. But I didn't see him. From time to time I drove my scooter between the car and the stairs and remembered journeys we had made as a family by car. Since there was no more room for me in the rear seat, a Dixan barrel was placed behind the front passenger seat so that I could sit on it. My father used to smoke while he was driving. Stuyvesant. For a moment it seemed to me that the aroma of his cigarettes, which I sometimes pulled for him at the vending machine, unfolded in my nose. I longed for him and it would have been nice if he'd come. But I didn't know where he was or when he came back.

While I was circling in front of the house, my mother suddenly appeared in the toilet window and shouted: "Don't drive between the car and the stairs, otherwise you'll break the car! Drive where there's plenty of room!"

She must have been watching me. Maybe we also agreed that I shouldn't get too far away from school.

"Yes, yes, I'll watch it!" I called back.

Then my mother disappeared again. I looked at the window and made sure she wasn't looking. Away from the car I made a few bends, stemmed the leg more strongly against the ground to get more speed, and then ran between the car and the stairs. I could put both feet on the scooter surface.

Due to the sufficient speed, the scooter gave me the feeling for a while that I was weightless and could move quickly without bending a single finger.

In the beginning I made my loops arbitrarily, by approaching the car sometimes from the front, sometimes from behind. I drove circles, ovals, slalom - what the trees were best suited for.

To increase the degree of difficulty, I tried to make the left turns smaller and smaller after passing the front right fender. This became more and more a balancing act. On the one hand I needed enough momentum not to touch the ground with my feet while driving through, on the other hand I could not have too much speed not to be carried out of the bend.

I could brake with the scooter, but I would have had to balance the manoeuvre. First of all the scooter had neither a rear nor a front mudguard - where the brakes were - due to its age and secondly I could not have put my right foot back to brake during the drive through: you lose your swinging balance and could get into a spin.

So I had to trust my steering skills. Several journeys were made until I suddenly slipped away in the final bend on the gravel ground. I fell, hit my knees and shortly afterwards I noticed that my right hand was bleeding heavily. Both knees were scratched.

I cried out in shock and pain and began to cry. My mother must have heard that.

She looked out the window, saw my heavy bleeding hand and came down immediately.

First she said a Band-Aid would do. But after we had arrived upstairs and she had connected me with gauze, she quickly decided to go with me to Dr. Bergmann, who had his practice in his own house.

We took the narrow path towards the church and had to ring the bell privately, because the consultation hour started later. He bandaged my hand, gave me a tetanus shot in the thigh and decided that we had to go to the hospital in Kürstadt.

I told my father to take us there.

My mother and I went home in a hurry. Where my father suddenly came from, I didn't know. There was no phone at school. He said he had been with Miss Grewen - who lived on the edge of the village - and he had talked to her about her exam preparations. My father was her mentor.

The three of us drove to Kürstadt in the Llyod. The wound was burning and very painful. I cried in pain. Now blood came through the gauze. That scared me. Arriving at the hospital, the doctor briefly looked under the bandage and muttered something about an operation: "The tendon of my right ring finger had been severed by the fall because the scooter no longer had handlebar grips. The rubber grips were broken by the constant throwing of the scooter. This had allowed the remains to slide inwards and released the sharp tube ends of the handlebars. I had hurt myself at the right end of the pipe. I yelled more at the hospital. Several men and a nurse in white long coats came to me and wanted to drag me into the operating room. A room I'd never seen before. With a large round lamp on the ceiling, which carried several spotlights. Leather straps were attached to the side of the couch underneath. I only perceived that superficially.

I shouted and braced myself against the tugging of the doctors, who obviously had trouble with me.

A doctor told my parents to talk to me and tell me that it would all be over soon.

The less I would oppose it, the sooner I could have surgery and go home again.

But that didn't help. I kept screaming.

Then strong arms lifted me onto the couch, pushed me down and started strapping me down with the brown leather straps. I fidgeted and struggled, even when they had already tied me so tightly that I felt that I could no longer escape from this table. My parents left the operating room. I can't remember if I asked them for help or if they couldn't stand my screaming anymore.

Then someone pressed a pot-shaped device onto my face, always turning my head, which was not strapped down, back and forth to escape. The pressure was too strong. I

17

only saw the big operation lamp, then a transparent fleece, this coarse grid-shaped apparatus...

Shortly afterwards I smelled something unknown and some-one began to count. My powers left me.

When I woke up, I was lying in the back of the car listening to engine noises. We drove. I raised my right arm and saw a huge bandage on my hand. It was the hand I always sucked my thumbs on. Now the doctors had made me such a large bandage that I could no longer use my thumb for it. Only the ring finger was injured. Why did the doctors bandage the thumb? Should the surgeons have heard anything from my parents during the anesthesia? You've been trying to stop me from sucking for a long time. I've liked sucking my thumb ever since I could remember and missed it a lot.

Nevertheless, I wanted to suck my favourite thumb now, but that wasn't possible because the whole hand was wrapped.

I smelled her and I started crying because she stank so much. Then I sucked my left thumb, which didn't taste so good. Besides, he wasn't clean. My right thumb was always clean. Even when I had played in the sawdust box, the up-per part of the thumb was always sparkling clean.

I often had a wreath of dirt on the root of my thumb. But that didn't bother me. As long as I could suck my thumb.

It was my father who said the day after my accident: "Well, hopefully you'll stop sucking your thumbs. This would be a good opportunity, as long as it's the bandage."

After the bandage was removed, I sucked on my right thumb again.

My brother

Clemens and I, now eight years old, shared a room that was accessible from the kitchen. One bed each. On my side of the bed stood a large, white wardrobe in which our clothes

18

and bed linen were stored. In the corner - next to his bed - was a four-legged, rectangular table, with a crocheted blanket on it. It was my brother's school desk with a Grundig tube radio on it. In the evening it received English hits from Radio Luxembourg for Clemens on Midwave. That always sounded noisy. Sometimes you had to re-tune the transmitter to receive it better. My brother explained to me that it was not possible to listen to Radio Luxembourg on VHF, because the station was in a faraway foreign country.

For the English hits, you couldn't avoid pressing the Medium-wave-button. Fortunately, I didn't have to turn the knob long on this radio, because it had two scales and two red search marks. So you could always have your master transmitter set to VHF and Medium wave.

Radio Tele Luxemburg with Camillo Felgen and his Novesia gold nut advertising. Because of the noise, it seemed to me that Camillo was somewhere in space. Besides, I always thought the host had something to do with tires. I didn't understand the songs. They seemed strange to me because of the different language.

It was a radio with a magic green eye. His changes indicated whether a transmitter was clearly received. Ideally, the dark green areas formed a narrow cross and released light green fields.

That was fascinating for me.

I spent minutes kneeling in front of the table on a chair - at a very low volume - turning the transmitter knob and watching the movements of this magic eye. I could lose myself and dream.

To the left of the radio stood a wooden table lamp with a lampshade made of transparent foil layers and grasses. From a distance, the grasses looked as if they had been painted on. If the light bulb was lit and you were close to the lamp, it seemed objectlike: both natural and fake. But the eye did not deceive the spirit. The grasses had once lived. They have been dried and somebody had intended them for this lampshade in which they live on, so to speak.

There were evenings when I went to bed or had to leave earlier than usual. One evening, my brother was sitting at his desk studying. There was some book open, next to it a notebook, pens for writing or drawing. The table lamp was on and the radio was playing.

My brother had left the room and I got up just to see what he was learning there. I tried to read the open book, but there were no German words in it. So I went back to bed.

My brother came back and sat down again. With his back to me.

He was studying and I think it was very exhausting for him.

After some time he was ready, put on his pyjama and went to bed.

Then he asked if we'd play with the flashlight beams: The room is pitch dark, everyone has a flashlight. One starts and turns on his flashlight, directing the beam to the wall or ceiling. The opponent then directs his turned off flashlight to the point of light and if he thinks he is in cover with this point, he turns his flashlight on. If he scores, he wins. If he does not hit, it is the first player's turn again. He then chooses a new job in the room.

We also played the second variation: Both players turned on their lamps and chased their light points on the ceiling. Whoever gets the other one first wins.

Then we fell asleep. Noises in the kitchen woke me up. It was still dark. My brother breathed quietly. He hadn't been aroused by the voices. Like cotton wool, I heard what was being said in the next room.

"Why isn't Father here yet?" Veronica asked.

"He has something to discuss with Miss Grewen for school," my mother replied.

"But he does that a lot" she replied," and mostly in the evenings. What is there so often to do," my sister continued.

"Psst! Not so loud! You'll wake up your brothers and sisters! Miss Grewen and her father are preparing for another exam, which she will soon have to take."

"The night before yesterday I saw Miss Grewen's house hugging each other - is that also part of the exam preparation," Veronika asked.

Silence. I got up and walked quietly to the door.

Put my ear to it.

"Father fell in love with Miss Grewen, didn't he?" Veronica asked. "That's why he's less with us." - Silence.

"Oh, where do you think?" my mother said, "Besides, it's time for you to go to sleep, it's already late. Good night."

It was quiet again in the kitchen.

Father and Miss Grewen?

I didn't get that. It was true that he was rarely at home, but he often said that he had several meetings in the evening. Teacher training, youth work, church choir and double-headed evenings with influential men from Kleinenbach.

I didn't want to believe that my father had fallen in love with my class teacher of all people, with whom I was also in love. Besides, it made me sad that he turned his back on us.

First, I wanted to wake my brother up to ask him if that could be true. But I didn't. That night, I didn't fall asleep anymore.

The Flashlight

Organ builders were in the village church. I didn't know what that profession was. My father took me with him and showed me what they were doing. I wanted to ask him first if he had been with Miss Grewen. But I didn't dare. I also believed what my father told me about his professional activities.

Veronica must have seen another man.

21

The cladding of the organ was dismantled. Inside, lights were on, two men in overalls set the tones. I was surprised that they were working in the church and making noise. Was that allowed? When I entered a church, I always had to be quiet and was only allowed to whisper, if at all.

The thick lever of the foot pump was in the lower position. Weeks ago I had to press it because the electric blower motor for the air bellows was broken. An organist cannot play because the pipes are not supplied with air.

My father had taken me to the morning mass. I didn't know exactly what to do. He showed me the wide wooden lever and showed me - before the mass began - how he kicked it down several times with his foot, thereby pumping air into the bellows. The work looked hard. When I tried the foot, I failed. My leg power wasn't enough. So I had to throw myself with momentum on the lever so that it moved downwards at all.

My father said I could do it. I should - while he was playing - always make sure that there was enough air in the bellows, otherwise the played notes would start to tremble or the believers would not hear any music at all. I had to pump up to transformation, sermon and communion and was not allowed to make any noises in order not to disturb the process. After that, I was very tired.

The organ builders used flat flashlights that shone brightly and that I had never seen before. With a kind of buttonhole: a leather piece with hinge, which looked like the end piece of very old suspenders. At first I thought the factory workers did something wrong because they attached suspenders to a flashlight. An organ builder enlightened me. You can hang the torch at chest height on a button of your working clothes and have both hands free. That's what he did to me.

I was very pleased with this torch, because it was characterized by another secret: one did not find immediately - like with a normal torch - the switch for switching on and off. I liked it so much because it made this lamp different from others. So I asked my father if he could ask an organ builder. The mechanic could then bring me a new lamp next time. I wanted to buy it from my pocket money if it wasn't too expensive. It was a black flashlight with a large reflector.

Brand Daimon 412.

An organ builder said, "Yes", which made me happy. Unfortunately the mechanics were not often in the village, so that I had to wait for months longingly for the lamp. Soon I didn't believe I'd ever get one.

In spring the organ builders were back again and one of them had even thought of the flashlight. I was very happy about that. My schoolmates, to whom I showed the flashlight the next day, looked for the switch on it. Many found it only with my help, because they switched it on by turning the reflector.

Vormstein

In the third and fourth grade my teacher was Miss Vormstein. An old woman who worked as a teacher because there were too few young teachers. It was a mystery to me why a 67-year-old girl let me talk to Miss. Given her age, I would have called her a woman. She seemed like a grandma to me. She showed this by her walking movements, which resembled those of the film Miss Marple, Margaret Rutherford. But Fräulein Vormstein was by far not so charming. Not a film detective, but an authoritarian teacher.

My brother was playing a soccer game alone on the schoolyard when Miss Vormstein came home with bags from shopping. By a stupid coincidence a shot ball flew in her direction and hit her at the bosom, which was not small.

23

Miss Vormstein blushed and was beside herself. She imme-diately confronted my brother. Then she complained to my mother and told her that Clemens had deliberately shot her the ball on her breasts. It could also cause breast cancer. My mother defended my brother, but mentioned this incident again and again in his presence and in the presence of others. Clemens was ashamed during these repetitions whe-re my mother grinned gloatingly.

I asked my mother why Fräulein Vormstein could be called Fräulein. Whether this applies only to us children or also to other people in the village.

"She's trying to show that she wasn't or isn't married. She has no children either," my mother replied. "She's what everyone calls her."

Gertrud Grewen was a lady to me because she was young. Teacher Vormstein was more than 50 years older than me and could not be a Fräulein. Fräuleins were 23 years old for me at the most. No way older.

The elderly teacher lived in the same school as me. Same floor. We lived next door to each other. It was not enough to show her respect and courtesy during the lessons, but to make matters worse, I did so during my free time, because I met her in the house.

In addition, Fräulein Vormstein occasionally asked for help when it came to hanging curtains or getting some eggs from the grocer.

In autumn Fräulein Vormstein had rung our doorbell in the evening and my mother had opened. She said she heard a strange rustling under the bed and she needed my help.

Since I was her student, it was hard for me to say no. I'm sure it would have had a negative effect on my grades. Miss Vormstein said she had placed a mousetrap under her bed a few weeks ago, but did not dare to look. I'd never dealt with mice before. Fear sneaked up on me. What if there wasn't a mouse in the trap? Or the mouse was in a corner under the bed? And she robs me the minute I look after the trap?

My mother told me to help Miss Vormstein. I felt miserable. I didn't mean to. But two teachers asked for it. Would I meet their expectations well? Would I get grades for my behavior? I've been observed and evaluated.

I hesitantly fetched my organ builder's torch, entered the neighbouring apartment after the two women, passed the bathroom, the door of which was half open, and glanced inside. Fräulein Vormstein's dental prosthesis, which she must have forgotten in a hurry, floated on the shelf in front of the mirror in a water glass. The teacher quickly closed the bathroom door and showed us the way to the bedroom. Besides the bed there was an oil stove, a wardrobe, a bookshelf and an old armchair. At first I kept my distance from her sleeping place and looked carefully around the room.

Listened.

Then I lay down in front of my bed, my flashlight turned on. My eyes followed the ray of light that illuminated the dusty ground. I tried to remember when I saw a live mouse. I didn't know. I didn't know. I don't think I ever have. What would a trapped mouse look like? Would she still be in the trap, fidgeting? Torment yourself, perhaps? Ask me for help to be freed? What would I do if she was motionless clamped?

At the back foot of the bed frame I discovered the mousetrap. But no mouse in the cone of light! Lucky for me. It's for me. Not for Miss Vormstein, who stood in the room full of expectation. "Can you see her?" my mother asked.

"No, there's nothing here," I replied, crawling out from under the bed with relief.

A few days later Miss Vormstein checked her homework. This time, a selection of children should step in front of the class and recite the passage from a book that we had borrowed for the first time from the school library that was in the vicarage. This kind of homework was new for us.

Several children were called. I was sitting in one of the back rows of benches. The teacher was initially satisfied with the children from the front rows. Since I understood the contents of the book that I had to borrow only fragmentarily, I did not have the courage to stand in front of the class and retell something.

Fortunately, I remembered a shoelace trick. Since the ends of the shoelaces were very long, I could step with the left shoe on the shoelace end of the right shoelace. Shortly thereafter I moved my right foot to the right and reached it by opening the loop of the left laces. The idea was brilliant.

At the moment when one pupil had finished his oral retelling and Miss Vormstein was looking for the next, I bent down skilfully and seemingly completely unexpectedly to restore my well-groomed appearance. Several times this trick succeeded. Meanwhile, I was so slow that I didn't have to go through the procedure a second time: while bending under the table, I listened spellbound to see which child was next. I was faking a tie, though. The shoelace remained untied especially for the next times.

In the course of one of my binding actions, Fräulein Vormstein suddenly shouted: "Thomas, what are you doing?"

I was scared, because I hadn't expected that. Why didn't Fräulein Vormstein accept that I was busy and had no time for a retelling? Before I could get to the front, my shoelace would have to be tied up so that I would look good and would not stumble. Should she have figured me out, or was that just a coincidence?

She said I could tie the tie in peace and she would ask another student to come forward. Afterwards I have to be ready and can step in front of the class. I would also have the opportunity to collect myself and tell a nice story to the

26

class. Miss Vormstein had actually caught me! She hadn't interpreted my signals the way I had intended her to.

Was Miss Vormstein forgetful? I had been looking for a mouse in her apartment and had helped her. That was an extra service. She should have left me alone about it.

Tobias certainly didn't have to step in front of the class. He would have thought of a more plausible trick.

I felt sober and full of shame. Of course I do. She could judge me better. Better than any child. Because we lived under the same roof, she knew me privately. My father, as her superior and colleague, will have told her not to spare me in class. Maybe she was afraid of his authority?

It went through me a freezing shiver. What was I supposed to do? To take the book now and read it quickly would be shameful. The remaining children would interpret it as a homework assignment not made. It would also be unfair to them. You didn't have that chance. Moreover, I would not have understood the text if I had been in such a hurry. What was to be done? I became more and more uncomfortable. Only now did it occur to me that I didn't have the book with me. Only a few more seconds separated me from my embarrassment. That was worse than detention with Miss Grewen. After all, I was older now, in a higher class, knew more and could read better.

Could I really read better? Although I was in the fourth grade, the children of the lower classes cut me down to it, but could I really do what I pretended to do? Or was that just a deception?

That stupid book I hadn't even picked out myself! The teacher had chosen it for me. I didn't want to borrow a book.

Right in the first chapter people falling into the house with the door. How would that work? Falling into the house with the door? I didn't get that. But I tried to visualize it: people come to a house, knock or ring the bell. However, it is not opened. So they take a running jump and run to the door, with such strength that they fall into the hallway with her!

Who should come up with the idea of destroying other people's doors in this way? And who would pay for the damage? Is it civilised to open doors like that? What would the homeowners say?

Questions after questions to which no one could answer me now. I didn't like this book: it had a dust jacket made of blue paper. Dark blue.

The pages of the book were yellowed. Moreover, it smelled of this dust, the books that stood for many years and were not used, unfold when you open them again.

The work was lying on my bedside table by the bed after I borrowed it. My mother asked if it was a book from the library. I affirmed and told her I should read it for class. The first chapter. And we should recount the contents of the first three pages. In addition to the other homework assignments. I rarely looked into the book. Its thickness and the small letters kept me from it. So far we haven't had the task of reading such thick books.

My pre-feed counter was ready. Miss Vormstein asked me. My shoelace trick wasn't an alibi anymore. With my head bowed, I shuffled slowly forward, now and then shyly looking at the teacher in the hope that she would read the ignorance of the contents from my face and save me and herself a disgrace in front of the class by asking her to sit down again. But that didn't happen. She didn't recognize my signals. I crossed my hands behind my back and stood there bent. Silent minutes passed. For me, terrible minutes in which everyone looked at me and waited for me to finally begin. I didn't know what to do at all. I only thought compulsively of this sentence again and again: Fall into the house with the door.

It was repeated by my memory as if it had no other chance of survival. As if it needed this sentence to perceive anything at all. As hard as I tried, I couldn't think of anything else. I started stammering after a while: "People falling into the house with the door..."

28

I kept remembering that one sentence. The first one I pronounced. But without any connection. Neither what people appeared in the book, nor what they did, nor who they talked to. Then there was silence again. I waited.

Fräulein Vormstein felt my insecurity. It was the first time for me that I stood in front of a class and had to retell something. My classmates who recounted before me could tell something. They had done their homework and understood their books.

Then the teacher broke the deadly silence. "What else did you read? What do you remember?"

I looked embarrassed to the floor. As if I could find an answer there. I couldn't remember. Don't concentrate.

Then Miss Vormstein explained the sentence to us children. Most of them couldn't do anything with it. This gave me the opportunity to take a breather and think up a plausible excuse for not knowing. But this compulsive search for a lied excuse put me in even greater distress. So in those seconds I not only searched for fragments from the book, but was increasingly never-pressed.

How could I find a plausible excuse under this time pressure?

I'm sure Tobias would have had one ready. My blood went into my head, my face swelled. I could feel his blush. Now a lie would be immediately transparent as a lie. I wish I was somewhere else. Far away from here.

No, I didn't want to go back to my seat in the bank either. What shame! What observation! I couldn't even relax my tension by rocking my feet or legs, even flailing or knocking with my arms and hands.

Paralyzed, I stood in front of the blackboard and my classmates. Not far from the desk where Miss Vormstein sat.

I was not on the same level with her, because that would have made me even more insecure. Authorities who scrutinized me from the strong side and waited for answers that I did not know paralyzed me.

29

What could I do? Again this tense silence, even worse than at the beginning. I hoped that Fräulein Vormstein would add something to the sentence "With the door falling into the house" that could help me. From the book. Yeah, did she even know this book? Didn't she say earlier that she didn't know? Or had I not heard that, only thought it myself? But she was a teacher. As such, she had to know all the books. If she didn't know the book, how could she explain that sentence? I didn't get that.

Fear minutes again. This silence and my speechlessness would last too long for her. She's gonna ask questions. Questions about the book. The content, the people, the story.

Since I couldn't give her an answer, she would eventually ask me if I had read the book at all. It was a homework assignment for today. That's what she would have said. Other children had already told about their books standing in front of the class.

I was most afraid of the question of whether I had read the first chapter. I didn't want her to catch me. The sentence With the door falling into the house was on the first page. I didn't understand him, he irritated me, so I didn't read on.

I was mute.

I didn't say sorry. I couldn't think of any. Not even the excuse that I couldn't talk right now came across my lips. My mouth was dry, my throat closed, my head lowered. I didn't want to look at anyone.

I was sweating. How could I succeed in freeing myself from this embarrassing situation? I didn't know. I didn't know. As I stood in front of the class for the first time, I had no experience and no means. It was one of those moments you curse to the extreme. From which one could not escape. All that remained was the hope that the martyrdom would not last long.

Lord, let the cup pass me by.

Then she asked, "Thomas, have you ever read the first pages?" I still didn't have an apology ready. So I acted as if she had ripped me mentally with her question out of an exhausting text search. I let my head jump up, but out of embarrassment I didn't turn it to her. At that moment, I couldn't look her in the eye.

Now I had to have an explanation. Stealthily and more out of reflex I nodded quickly.

Another long pause. My nod had given me time to think. But only a short one. Cause I didn't say anything. An immediately pronounced, plausible apology would have saved me more. I felt it at that moment. This short, almost indistinct nod was too passive.

Waiting. Anxious waiting. Miss Vormstein waited, her classmates waited. Some got bored. It's the seconds that can paralyze an entire class with a teacher. I looked down again. Looking for excuses there. My head was empty. Absolutely empty. I didn't dare lie. She would have noticed. A lie must sound true to be true.

My old teacher would know it right away. She had a lot of life experience.

Waiting. It's that waiting again. Miss Vormstein became impatient.

I swallowed hard.

I speculated that she would assume that I had read the book, understood it and kept it, but now here, in front of her and the class, I had no courage to talk about it.

Waiting. Seconds. minutes.

"What kind of people are there in this book?" asked Miss Vormstein. "What are they doing?"

I breathed flat. Nothing, nothing occurred to me. I had only opened the book a few times, read a few sentences, not understood and then closed it again. Then put it back on my bedside table.

There it was now.

"Are there children in the book? What are they doing? Do they play anything?" she insisted further.

In the days after the loan I had completely forgotten that we should retell the content. This morning, right at the first hour, the teacher asked us to do this. So it was too late for me to read the chapter and keep it.

So what could I do?

I didn't know. I didn't know.

I was at a loss.

"Did you read the book too?" she asked again.

I nodded again and knew at that moment that this was my excuse for lying.

Silence.

"Either you didn't read it or you can't talk about it now. I'll give you time until the next German lesson to read the chapter again and then retell it here. Now's the time to listen to your classmates retell."

I stayed silent. I couldn't imagine being saved for the moment. In thought, I apologized to the teacher.

But I never wanted to hear that story again. Fall into the house with the door. And don't read either, because reading small print caused me a lot of trouble.

My classmate Bernd, child of a farmer, could already read the daily newspaper, that was the word in the village. What about me? As the main teacher's son, I was not even able to re-count the first chapter of a children's book! What a Blamage!

"Thomas, you can sit down again," said Miss Vormstein. This sentence slowly worked for me.

Then I felt I could walk and I did. I went to my seat, sat down and was taken. I didn't get the rest of this hour despite being asked to. That burdened me, because I was supposed to learn how to retell like my classmates.

The Pumpkin

"We recently read the story about the pumpkin," said Miss Vormstein as she bent over and fiddled with her bag, lifted something out and placed it on the desk. "This preserving jar with pumpkin pieces is from my sister, whom I recently visited in Staffelberg. Every year she cooks pumpkin and gives me a few glasses.

Yesterday I asked you to bring bowls and spoons so we could try pumpkin today.

Did you bring your things?"

My classmates unpacked their eating utensils immediately. I was the only one who didn't have anything. I was ashamed of it.

Probably would affect my grade.

At the same time I was happy because I did not want to eat pumpkins from strangers. Neither Miss Vormstein nor her sister, whom I did not know. Besides, I didn't find the pieces in the glass appetizing.

Fräulein Vormstein opened the preserving jar, asked us children to go forward and filled something in small bowls. I stayed seated. It was all right with me that she was busy and therefore didn't immediately notice that I hadn't gone to the desk with her. Little by little the children sat down again and began to eat. Miss Vormstein filled herself up a little. Then she looked at us.

"Where's your little bowl?" she asked me.

I flashed red. Now I couldn't hide anymore.

"Did you forget?"

I looked down and nodded stealthily.

She shook her head.

"But I told you yesterday I'd bring pumpkin and think of the bowls and spoons."

It didn't occur to me to be able to run quickly upstairs and bring the things. But by the time I got back, the children would have finished eating and I would have delayed the lessons. Fräulein Vormstein would certainly not like that, because I disturbed her lesson planning.

In addition, there was certainly no one in the apartment. Neither my brothers and sisters nor I had a key. My parents were against it. My mother had probably gone shopping. Before admitting to her that I had forgotten my bowl and spoon, I would also have been punished.

My father taught himself. The higher classes. In this school. Sometimes he also had substitute lessons in the lower classes. But I'd never visited him in his class before. I haven't had the courage. Besides, I wouldn't have known what class he was in. I would have had to knock on all the doors to find him and disturb all the other teachers teaching.

I didn't dare knock on his class door and interrupt his lessons even now. In addition, older students would have seen me and I would have had to confess to my father in their presence that I needed small bowls and spoons for the pumpkin dinner at Fräulein Vormstein. I'm sure that would have made a laugh. Furthermore, my father would have had to suspend teaching in order to accompany me to the apartment, because I did not know where my head was in such moments.

Was my father even there today? I didn't know. I didn't know. He often took care of matters outside school.

For four years I didn't need any overgarments on my way to school, because I only had to go down one floor, pass through a door and shortly afterwards I was in my classroom. I didn't even have to go through the main entrance of the school - like my classmates. That might sound like an advantage. If I had forgotten books, notebooks or writing utensils, I could have fetched them quickly.

It would also have been possible to play in the classrooms in my spare time.

But my parents forbid it.

The fact that I was in a school day and night was depressing. I couldn't get away from her, never get away from her in my spare time. Never look at the school from another perspective. How my classmates did it. They went to school every day. To the building and back. They could fax or pull on teachers. But a main teacher's son is not suitable for listening on the way to school.

I was not able to establish social contacts on my way to school during these years. In addition, I received few visits from friends at home. What should encourage students to go to school in their free time?

Children are very reluctant to visit a main teacher's son because they do not know whether children's secrets that a teacher's son could pass on to his father-teacher are exchanged while playing - and the latter then uses them against the pupil.

Perhaps Miss Vormstein had also acted arbitrarily and we were not allowed to eat in class? And pumpkins from strangers?

Maybe I would have betrayed her at my father's by bowl-spoon-holing and she would have gotten into trouble with him? This could have a negative effect on my grades.

But since Miss Vormstein lived with us under the same roof, she would certainly talk to my parents about bowls and spoons.

Private. Not through the teacher's room.

My classmates ate. Time passed. Then Miss Vormstein said to me: "I'm going to eat my pumpkin pieces and then you can have my little bowl and spoon to eat the pumpkin with it".

Nausea crept up on me. I couldn't say anything. I should eat off her dishes? Washed up? That old woman's dishes? I didn't want to taste the pumpkin. Now it occurred to me that I did not like pumpkin, although I had never tried it before.

I watched Miss Vormstein eat. She put the spoon in her Omamund. It was a plastic spoon. I remembered someone once telling me that plastic spoons could never be cleaned like metal spoons. Bacteria would always stick to them. Even after thorough rinsing. I didn't want to eat from an old teacher's dishes.

"Do you like it, kids?" she asked.

The class nodded. Probably couldn't afford an honest sentence. Finally Fräulein Vormstein had made every effort to transport the pumpkin glass. She didn't have a license or a car. She was on trains, buses and black taxis. Since her sister lived in a city, our teacher had to laboriously transport the glass. She would have been offended if people had said, "I don't like your pumpkin!"

This would certainly have had a negative effect on the grade. I got worse. I should eat off her dishes? With her plastic spoon? I couldn't resist your suggestion. Because of the note. I had to join in. Even though I was disgusted at the thought of eating from her dishes. I didn't like pumpkins. Especially not from her. What if she handed me the dishes filled with new pumpkin pieces at the end of her meal? Untreated? And the spoon you used? I couldn't argue with her. Should have reluctantly eaten the pumpkin from her used dishes out of guilt.

Miss Vormstein ate the last pieces.

Then she stood up: "I wash the bowl and the spoon in the toilet. Please be quiet for so long." She left the room.

What if she didn't flush the things at all and came back after a short time? Or if she only dried the dishes and the spoon with a cloth? Or there wouldn't be any water in the toilet, by any chance? There was no dishwashing liquid.

She came back. Filled pumpkin pieces into the bowl and brought them to me. The other kids were almost done. I was ashamed because I delayed the progress of the lesson. Besides, they'd all be looking over at me. I didn't want to eat among gawking people. I'd rather eat unobserved. As long as people eat, they're more concerned with themselves. Very few people like to be watched. Unless the observers eat too.

But as soon as they're done, they'd rather stare - like others eat.

The bowl was in front of me. The spoon was next to it.

Both seemed to be washed up. Anyway, the spoon was dry. The bowl too.

Outside. - I hesitated.

Miss Vormstein saw that. And I didn't want to disappoint her. Slowly I took the spoon, dunked it in the juice, loaded a piece of pumpkin and led both to my mouth. The pumpkin looked pink. I knew melon. Watermelon. I've tried these before. It tasted sweet. I was hoping this pumpkin tasted as sweet as a melon. Someone once told me that pumpkin and melon were related. However, I had eaten the melon raw. Not boiled melon.

The spoon was in my mouth. Disgusted me. I was thinking of her wrinkled Omamund and her denture prosthesis in the glass, which was now probably stuck to her palate with adhesive powder. I was thinking that this spoon had touched her prosthesis a few minutes ago. The pumpkin biscuit was on my tongue. Along with the juice, it tasted salty. I didn't like it. It tasted very different from a melon.

Slowly I chewed the piece. Swallowed carefully. Hesitantly, I took the next one. She had filled the bowl. I should eat all that? My stomach cramped up. I didn't dare tell her that. I was ashamed. I had forgotten my own dishes and spoon, now my teacher and my classmates were waiting for me to eat quickly. And I would refuse? Again I saw the picture of the pumpkin-eating teacher in front of me. I wish I'd thought of my own bowl!

Now I was going fast. Like taking a bad-tasting drug. I ate faster and choked down the pumpkin pieces almost unchewed. I left the juice in the bowl. Miss Vormstein got her things and said, "Did you like it?!"

I looked down and nodded embarrassed.

Mark

In the big break there were classmates and me behind the school building and Ulrich wanted to catch me. But we weren't allowed to play hunting because the whole schoolyard was split. I didn't want to get caught and ran away by running through groups of students standing around. The best escape destination seemed to me to be the front of the school. So I ran near the house wall around a corner that I couldn't see and collided with Markus, the son of a doctor, who happened to come running from the other side. Unfortunately, I fell. I cried, my knee started to bleed and hurt.

Miss Grewen, who was in charge of the breaks, came from afar and scolded both of us.

While someone informed my mother about the fall, Markus invited me to his home. For next week. To play with. I found that unusual, because he wasn't in my class. It's a deeper one. He was younger. We'd never played together before. I was all the more surprised by his invitation.

I had no more lessons.

Teacher Schommer had fetched the dark brown leather bandage bag with the red cross and had tied my knee makeshift. During the break I was supposed to go to Markus' father's practice - because of the dirt that was in the wound. Miss Grewen said I had to get a shot, "You're fine," said some classmates who hurried up and watched, "You're off." But I would have preferred to go to class because I was afraid of the doctor and the syringe.

My mother came, looked at the connected knee and we immediately went to Dr. Bergmann.

The knee was bleeding badly. It was an emergency. That's why I got it right away. The doctor applied iodine to the wound, bandaged it and told me to clench my teeth. Then he gave me a shot in the right thigh. That hurt more than the wound on the kneecap. My mother and I slowly went home.

After Markus had opened my front door on the day of my invitation, he asked me how I was doing. Then he showed me his toys. I'd never seen anything like it before. A large basement room full of toys: baseball bats, rubber balls, flummeries, cars with remote control, model airplanes, a chain car, a table tennis table with bats and balls, soccer shoes, three leather soccer balls, two bicycles, a rubber dinghy, a badminton game, a throwing game with arrows, a Carrera racecourse, a larger box with matchbox cars. In addition card games: the fastest ships, the fastest cars, old-timer quartet, Elferraus.

Markus was an only child.

And doctor's son.

I didn't even know where to look first. He already asked me what we wanted to play with. I should choose something, because it's the first time I've been with him.

I would have liked to have driven the Kettcar. I've wished for it many a time for Christmas. But it was too expensive for my parents. "You've got a bike," they said, "you can ride it around the same way." But now, with my knee injured, I couldn't ride a bicycle or a chain car.

The amount of toys overwhelmed me. I couldn't make a decision.

"How about," Markus asked, "if we played with my railroad?" "Railway?" I said, "but I don't see any railway!" "Here in the other room." He opened a door and we went next door. I saw a giant railroad plate. Much bigger than the one we had. And with many more points, signals, mountains, transformers, houses, rails, tunnels, cranes, cars, roads, trains, depots. As soon as Markus had turned on the main switch, the many plastic houses lit up. "I'm taking this locomotive here," he said. That's how we played until I had to go home.

But Markus was never a close friend. He was often polite. Just a son of a doctor. Besides, a school class under mine. I preferred to play with those who were in my class. With Tobias, who in autumn built 'huts' out of leaves, hid in them and blinded the passing drivers with a triple lamp.

Or with Jürgen, who was one of the strongest in the class. He usually wore three-quarter leather pants. Not the green ones, made of smooth leather, the grey ones, made of rough leather. And thick stockings.

Jürgen always collected beads from empty ink cartridges during his lessons. From Geha or Pelikan - he didn't care. He cut off the lid at the end of the cartridge with the sharpener, pushed the case open on the table until the bead fell out, took a cartridge that already contained several beads and inserted this new bead in the front. He did it by putting his ball depot cartridge upside down on the ball and pushing vigorously. He asked everyone for empty cartridges.

I couldn't give him any. Cause I had an old fountain pen. With piston. Every afternoon I checked if there was enough ink in the tank, because I was embarrassed not to be able to write with him in class.

If possible during a class test. Occasionally I had a small bottle of royal blue ink with me. But it was always very cumbersome. And since the day when the lid of the bottle once jumped off, when it was in its knapsack and bruised books and notebooks, I avoided taking it with me.

How I wished for a fountain pen with bullets, but my parents were against it. It was too expensive for them. Besides, there'd be plenty of old piston fillers in my dad's desk drawer, they said. Some were from pen representatives, others from my siblings or my grandpa. But very few of them worked properly.

It was summer. I rode my bike along the narrow footpath towards the archery hall. No reason. It's a pastime. Or perhaps because I was curious about what was going on at the archery place, because the village shooting match was imminent and carnies had travelled there.

I came over the small wooden pedestrian bridge, drove past the shooting hall and saw the little booths, the car scooter course, merry-go-rounds whose construction elements were assembled and which gradually took shape. Fitters were wearing steel bracing. The men seemed dirty and run-down. Some had unkempt faces. One was missing a tooth. I could see it when they talked to each other and laughed at something. Trucks with open hatches stood around. Tools and individual parts for assembly were scattered around the site.

I kept my distance from strangers and objects. My boredom was paired with the curiosity to see what was going on there.

Maybe I could watch if the men drove the bumper cars without chips. I happened to see that before. They had a U-shaped plastic key, with a thick, ball-shaped key fob on it, as you know it from hotel keys. Except there wasn't a number on that tag.

As soon as they had let the cars from the transporters onto the steel platform of the scooter, which were mounted at the top with arched current collectors and the current flowed through the wire net, the men sat down on the entry edge of the cars, a foot to accelerate inwards and a leg outside on the thick rubber lip, put their special keys into the chip slot and drove off. Often, one hand casual on the pantograph rod and the other hand on the steering wheel. Before I realized for the first time that these men used a special key to drive, I had always suspected that they would have to earn a lot of money in their profession so that they could buy the chips to drive to move and try out the wagons.

My pocket money wouldn't have been enough for that. After all, there will have been about twenty or thirty scooters coming from the trucks there.

In any case, I had often wished to have such a universal key, which I could then use every time after the opening of the shooting match.

With that I would have driven endlessly long bumper cars without having to spend a penny of my money.

I got on my bike and kept going. First towards the sports field, then back again to see if the men were sitting on their scooters and driving in the meantime. Sometimes, when the boss didn't look or have anything to do, they took the liberty of having fun. They showed all their skill with these cars. They were driving close to the gangway or were holding at full throttle, only to turn the wheel around at the last moment, so that the reverse gear was engaged. Sometimes my breath faltered, because I thought: he drives directly in front of the wooden gang and is thrown out of the car at the end, because he only sits with one half of his body on the car!

After the opening of the shooting range it is forbidden to sit on the wagon like this. Visitors were immediately reprimanded by the servants if they did so. Still, I remembered some adolescents who did that anyway. They sat with their butts on the back of the scooter, so they could overlook the field better and especially impress the girls. However, this can only be done by adolescents who are young enough, because one foot must reach the accelerator pedal. Individual mechanics were holding their cars towards each other and then pulled the wheel aside at the last moment so as not to collide with their colleague. Often they also piloted an unmanned car into the corner where it was parked.

They did this by driving their car alongside them, grabbing the wheel of the other car and then accelerating their car.

What impressed me most about the men was that they mastered reversing with these cars. But not at crawl speed, at full throttle. By just watching, I learned from them how to do that. They were moving forward a bit at first. Then turned the steering wheel 180 degrees. And very quickly, so the car wouldn't make a bend. Then they held the wheel in this position and drove backwards.

The attraction of this reverse driving lies on the one hand in the backward movement and on the other hand in the steering action. You have to think backwards. Because if I now turn the steering wheel to the right, in the hope that the car will then make a right turn, I quickly learn better: the car will make a left turn. Of course, seen in the rear driving direction. Such unexpected manoeuvres could quickly lead to collisions as soon as one tried out these driving skills after the opening of the shooting match.

It was interesting, if you wanted to avoid a forward driving person while reversing: then you often steered in the opposite direction and it came to a collision.

The fitters were able to reverse full pirouettes on the steel and elegantly intercept the car. They had the most modern hits played and the music sounded loud all over the place.

That was what made the atmosphere for these experts so special.

What I liked the most was when three or four people were driving the steel platform at the same time, almost faking collisions and then professionally dodging them. Maybe they had secretly placed bets on whether someone would let themselves be caught by any tricks.

I wish I could drive like this. But there were many more wagons on the steel field during the festival than there are now. In addition, reversing drivers were asked to drive forwards by the cashier via loudspeakers. There were often unpredictable clashes by adolescents who ignored the driving rules.

The assembly activities on the shooting range fascinated me more, so that I stopped with my bicycle to observe the scenery more calmly and more exactly. For this I leaned sideways against the bicycle bar, so that the bicycle served as a support and let my gaze wander.

Suddenly a man called me to him. I was frightened because I was thinking and did not expect to be approached from a distance. I hesitated not to assess this signal. He called again. Now I couldn't avoid it anymore. Although I didn't want to go to his place, I did.

When I faced him, he asked me if I had time. I said, "Yes." He kept asking if I could do him a favor. I affirmed that too, although I had long since said no inside. My mother had always warned me about strange men. Now I was paralyzed. The man told me that he had ordered groceries from Hausmanns for his colleagues and himself. I'm sure I'd know Hausmanns. He had not been able to take the things with him because the carton had to be packed first. Now the box must be ready for collection. In addition, the food was already paid for. But he didn't have time to get them himself and neither did his men. If I had time, I should do it and choose a chocolate or something else as a reward for my efforts. I don't need to carry the box either, because I can put it on the back of the carrier.

The man told and told.

I said yes, just to be helpful. And not to be taken for an idiot. I didn't want to drive. But when I had said yes, but actually meant no, I could hardly say no afterwards, because I had learned to obey adults and not to contradict them.

I drove off, but I didn't know exactly what to do. A voice inside me shouted, "No!" I had never done anything like this before and I didn't know if his story was really true. What if he was fooling me with it? Or what if I went to Hausmanns and nobody there knew about a box? Then what was I supposed to do? I didn't know the man's name. He didn't tell me. And I had forgotten to ask in the excitement. How should I explain myself to Mrs. Hausmann?

I turned into this road, then into that road. But the roads didn't lead to Hausmanns. Sweat broke out on my forehead. What if the man waited now and wondered where I was for so long? Hausmann's business was not far from the rifle range. About ten minutes on my bike.

I kept thinking about why the man didn't drive to the store himself. He mentioned he didn't have time. And neither are his men. Should I believe him? What was I supposed to do? The minutes passed and the man waited for me.

With him his colleagues, who were undoubtedly hungry from work and wanted something to eat.

If I wasn't back in a reasonable time, he might think I sold the stuff. Or have an accident. With all the food. An accident! I could have called him and told him I wasn't picking up his box.

Did he have a phone in his trailer? I didn't know. I didn't know.

It suddenly occurred to me that I did not know how to use the telephone, as we did not have a private telephone. The school didn't even have an affiliation. Even coin-operated phones were strangers to me. Would I have had any money for that? And his phone number?

What was I supposed to do?

The only way seemed to me to go home and tell my mother about the encounter. To ask your advice. Although I was afraid of their reaction, because I should not talk to foreign men, let alone carry out orders for them.

I only saw this solution, even if it meant that the men had to wait longer on the square.

So I drove home. My mother was there. I told her the story. She was horrified at my actions, wanted accurate information. I told her what I knew. What was I supposed to do? My despair grew. My mother advised me to get the box from Hausmanns - because I had said yes - to take him to the

45

shooting range and come home immediately. And above all, not to accept anything from the man or other people. No money, no food. And I should tell him that in the future I wouldn't get any boxes or anything else for him or any other people.

Stitches in the stomach.

I hoped my mother would talk to the man immediately and make sure that he took care of the box himself. If that wasn't possible, I wish that my mother would keep me at home, so that the case would be solved differently. The men would then have to take care of their own food. But I shouldn't be allowed to be seen in the firing range anymore. Neither today nor during the shooting festival. They would recognize me and address me. You'd get mad at me. Blame me. I probably shouldn't be driving that bumper car. That's what I wanted.

Reluctantly, I went to Hausmanns in a flash. What if I met my client in the shop because I hadn't brought the box yet? He wouldn't like that, and I'd have to justify myself to him. I wouldn't get my reward. And drive a bumper car?

What if the food had actually not been paid for and the owner refused to give it to me?

"Hello, Thomas," she said.

"Hello," I replied, looked at her shyly and said after a while: "A man from the shooting festival sent me. I'm supposed to get a box..."

She bent over and picked him up on the bar. The mechanic didn't get it himself.

"It's all paid for," she said and knew that the content was for the carnies and someone was coming. She was also informed about the gift. That was lucky for me, because otherwise I would have had to address them, which would have been unpleasant for me. Because I didn't know if the mechanic had told me the truth. Maybe the announced reward was just a lure for me to get the box. After all my mistakes, was I entitled to a gift at all?

46

Mrs Hausmann asked me what I wanted. I thought for a while, thinking whether I really didn't have to pay for the present or whether it was just a trick to lure me in for the job. I didn't have any money on me. It seemed to me that I was thinking too long and stole valuable time from the salesgirl. Her work at the store. I always felt worse. Gift or no gift.

After a while I remembered Capri ice cream. It was one of my favorite irons and I rarely got it because it was too expensive. This ice-cream on a stick had an orange or lemon flavour. I told Mrs. Hausmann I wanted that orange-flavored. She took it out of the freezer and put it on the counter.

After the shopkeeper and I had brought the full cardboard box to the bike and the luggage clip held it, I carefully leaned the bike against the wall and fetched the ice. When I went in, I remembered that I couldn't ride a bicycle with the ice. With this heavy cardboard box on the carrier I needed both hands on the handlebars, otherwise I would fall.

So what was I supposed to do? I stood there and pondered: I could put the ice on the box and eat it later. But the sun was shining very strongly. It could happen that the ice melts, the paper softens and the other objects smear. Then I'd probably have trouble with the mechanic. Worst-case scenario, I'd have to pay the groceries out of my pocket money.

I wouldn't have any of my gift - the ice cream. I would have to hurry with the cardboard transport and would be therefore still more hurried, than I was it anyway by the time delay. Consequently, this meant a renunciation of the ice. I didn't like a melted ice any more.

I was thinking. Meanwhile I felt that Mrs Hausmann, who was standing at the bar again, was watching me through the big shop window. She hadn't decorated an area so she could always look outside and know what was happening in front of her store.

After a short time the saleswoman came to the store and said: "Eat your ice cream first, Thomas! Then you can drive off in peace."

I nodded embarrassed, but said nothing. She was right. But I was already late. What Mrs Hausmann didn't know. She must have assumed that I drove straight to her from the rifle range to pick up the box. She had no idea I was late. I hadn't told her because that would have cast a bad light on me. Out of shame, I didn't want to confide in her afterwards.

I said a quick, embarrassed "yes" to the shopkeeper so as not to get into trouble with her, my time and the ice.

Our family rarely bought from Hausmanns and it was unpleasant for me to have a longer conversation with her now. We only went into her shop when something was needed very urgently. That hardly ever happened. So I was surprised she gave me a tip for ice cream. She didn't have to do that because we weren't regulars. We always drove with our car to Kürstadt, there was not only the hospital where I was operated, but also the supermarket Hill.

It was bigger and had more food. In addition, in this supermarket one was not approached by the staff, because it was a self-service shop. Hausmann was a grocery store. If you had entered it, you had to talk to the owner immediately.

But she was a stranger to me.

Because we bought our food somewhere else, we were looked at crookedly in the village.

But I can't say that Mrs. Hausmann was rude to me. But I was late! What would the mechanic think of me?

The shopkeeper was right with her suggestion to first eat the ice cream and then transport the goods.

On the other hand, the man had been waiting longer for his things. In order not to disappoint the saleswoman, I pushed the ice out of the paper and began to suck on it. She took the trash with her and went back to her shop. Thus I had reached a small goal and satisfied Mrs. Hausmann. Showed her that her suggestion was probably the best. Otherwise she might have discussed it with me, which would have been very unpleasant for me.

The sun was shining very strongly.

It was hot in the small area in front of the shop window. The ice started melting faster than I liked. I licked it a few times hastily and panicked quickly. First it was no pleasure for me and second - and that was the worse - I thought of the box. Wasn't there butter in there that could melt just as fast? Or other perishable goods? Besides, I was already late! The mechanic would read me the riot act.

I had to go! With the ice! I couldn't stand here any longer and enjoy it while the man and his people waited for the box! They waited hungry for their food.

Eating ice cream and cycling at the same time would not work! With the heavy luggage in the back I needed both hands to steer. Otherwise I'd fall and there'd be a bigger mishap. In the end I would have to pay the useless food and additionally a carton with new food from my pocket money!

I didn't like throwing away the Capri ice cream. It was a gift! You don't do that with gifts! Besides, I wouldn't have had any of it. Lick three times, maybe. And that's my favorite ice cream. So I thought about what I could do now. I didn't want to ask Mrs. Hausmann. She was back in her business and was certainly busy.

A plan developed: I would first push the wheel a bit - with the ice in my hand and at the same time on the handlebar - so that Mrs Hausmann, who could see me through the shop window in any case, noticed that I was going out and carrying out my job properly. At the same time, she would think that I had found a compromise: I suck my ice cream and push my bike.

Parallel to these considerations I already saw myself throwing the almost complete ice stealthily into the next trash or into the ditch, only to arrive as quickly as possible at the shooting range with an undamaged karton and its contents.

It was warm, I was sweating, even out of panic, and I implemented my plan. I pushed the wheel, held the now dripping ice with two fingers on the stick and had both hands on the handlebars. In fact, Mrs. Hausmann looked through the shop window and nodded to me. I smiled embarrassed and nodded too.

The box was heavy. I felt the load and pushed my bike, which I had to constantly balance to prevent the box from slipping. I wished I could pedal because I had more strength with my legs.

The ice had to disappear as quickly as possible.

There were houses on the street and so I felt watched. Did I get to throw away the ice cream present? They didn't! And certainly not as a well-bred main teacher's son!

I looked unobtrusively from time to time from my corner of my eye along the houses. Always wondering if I could see someone watching me. There were no wastebaskets here. I don't like garbage cans either. But there were house free areas and partly ditches, which were overgrown with tufts of grass.

That would give us a chance.

A piece of road ditch in which the discarded ice would quickly melt in the sun and in the end only the wooden handle would remain, which after a good week would look so badly weathered due to the road dirt, as if it had been here for several years.

I saw a good spot on the left side of the road, crossed the road after a glance and threw the ice into the ditch. The throw succeeded as if the ice had accidentally and unintentionally fallen out of my hand. For a supposed observer should believe that an accident has happened to me.

From now on I could use both hands exclusively for steering. After putting the right pedal in a comfortable starting position, I got on the bike, kicked down the crank and started off with caution. Carefully I cycled to the man on the square and stopped. He took the box from my porter and put it on the floor. At the same time he asked me why the transport had taken so long. I mumbled something incomprehensible. I hadn't thought about making up an excuse first.

Suddenly my mother came and spoke indignantly to the man. What would come to his mind to hire boys to get food cartons. He could do this himself or one of his employees.

That was extremely unpleasant for me. It embarrassed me that I had let myself be persuaded by the mechanic and my mother and that it came now because of me to such inconveniences.

It was wrong to tell her about it. I already felt miserable because of the poorly executed order.

And the man was mad at me because I was late and my mother had turned it on. He'd remember my face and never give me a job like that again. Especially not a gift. It was also unclear whether I would ever be allowed to buy chips for the bumper car - let alone drive them. I'm sure he'd watch me more closely during the shooting match than the others.

The Confession

The village priest. Seedorn. One of the old school. Like so much in this village anyway.

He lived between the church and the school building in his office building.

An old, fat man, always dressed in black, even when he was doing his much-loved gardening. I wondered if he was also dressed dark in bed at night. With black pyjamas?!

Strange people like that. As if they were born in black clothes. That thought always made me very sad. I doubted whether clergy could ever laugh.

My mother said, "Of course they can laugh, they're people like you and me." That statement fed my doubts. People like you and me? A priest of this format? And anyway, why did this important teacher for me have to be so old? I didn't get that. No. I really didn't understand that. Reverend Seedorn. The man who was also responsible for communion and altar boy classes.

He was one of the strictest people I ever met as a child. I didn't notice it during the first masses I attended and which he celebrated. I sat as a young believer in the pew and saw him during his work only from a distance.

His severity was revealed when I had to attend communion class. The lessons took place in a cellar room of his office building which had been equipped for this purpose.

The clergyman was always walking around with a rubber truncheon. I didn't see that club on him at first. Older children had told me about it before, so I looked curiously when I would discover it.

He wore it under his frock. Or was it a cassock? Reverend Seedorn ran back and forth between the corridors of the benches. Asked some students about certain passages in the catechism and wanted to hear the Ten Commandments. Because I didn't know two, he hit me with his club on the fingers, which I had to stretch towards him. That was his standard punishment. Once upon a time a child was naughty, it was on his ass.

We Communion students all had respect for that rubber stick. This led me to learn the essentials, but out of fear of punishment I asked no further questions. I was very concerned about some of the questions.

The date of the first confession was approaching. The prerequisite for Holy Communion was the successful participation in it. That scared me, because in the confessional I had to reveal my sins to Father Seedorn. I found this idea worse than standing in front of the class of teacher Vormstein and having to retell the chapter of a book.

During my stay in the confessional cabin, I would not only be confronted with the clergyman as a testing authority, but also with God. That is: I kneeled across from them.

What should I do not to fail before Reverend Seedorn and before God?

I thought of writing down my sins to at least have a mind support in the confessional.

But also for the purpose of not being left empty-handed. Would Father Seedorn allow me to write down my sins?

And God? Or did I have to recite them out of my head? Would it be a sin to bring a note with you?

What an embarrassment! My friends might have had ten or even more sins, but my breath would have got stuck like a lump in my throat, because I was so nervous in the confessional - without notes - that only two sins would have occurred to me.

In response to the confessor's questions, I would have had only a shy shake of the head to answer.

I imagined all this in advance.

The decisive day was there. I had my list folded in my pocket. In the weeks since it was created, it was the most important thing I had to carry with me and I guarded it like the apple of my eye. This guarded list, which I would not even have entrusted to my mother to read, was to be destroyed in a secret place immediately after the great confession.

Still in the morning I tried to learn my sins by heart. With the fourth sin, I wondered if I should leave it on my piece of paper. I just had a hunch.

Neither in communion class nor anywhere else did I dare to ask. Although I always had the hope that a classmate would ask Father Seedorn and I could then benefit from the answer, this did not happen.

On the Friday before White Sunday all the children who were admitted to communion and who had to confess before sat on the pew. I wasn't quite at the end. I never liked the ends. You're the last one. The first ones are already in the triumphal frenzy and you don't get absorbed in it yourself. It's better to go down. Because you should never be happy as long as you're before the finish line.

I sat devoutly in the last third and watched closely how long my predecessors took in the confessional.

I looked into their faces after the visit. Some children seemed relieved. Most, however, were more concerned with themselves and their sins afterwards than before. That made me uneasy. What was I supposed to do? Was there a way back? A way out for me?

It was time. It was my turn. I stumbled nervously from the wooden base of the pews. Two, three steps to the confessional cabin, which was near the baptismal font in darkness.

What was I supposed to say, what did I have to say again? When entering the confessional? I was thinking...

Had all of that made me speechless?

Just a few more inches.

I knew the man in the confessional from communion class. I hope it was him, too! I hadn't seen him go into the confessional today. He must have entered it some time before us. Before we kids went to church.

But of course I knew him! He lived not far from our house. He'd come for a visit now and then. Mostly on special occasions. Last of all, my sister's communion. Or was it confirmation? Anyway, something important. Something that justifies a parish visit to a neighboring house.

I pushed the curtain aside. Shortly thereafter, a foot unexpectedly grazed the lower edge of the confessional when entering. I almost tripped. I recognized the knee-bench in a shadowy way. Trembling, I kneeled down. Now I couldn't see anything from the darkness. It made me more nervous.

It was not bright in the part of the church where we had waited on the benches. Here in the confessional, it was unexpectedly darker for me.

54

What was allowed, what had to be said again - when entering the confessional?

"Praise be to Jesus Christ," I said quietly.

"Forever and ever. Amen!" I was answered.

This dark confessional gave me the impression of death and destruction.

No light.

Silence.

Musty smell.

Is it possible to confess in the light, in the light? Do sins look different with brightness? Are there any sinners at all?

I looked through the perforated wood. I'd never seen the inside of a confessional before. I've passed him by reverently so far. I always believed that as long as one has not reached the age of a sinner, one need not concern oneself with confession.

For me, sinners could only be adults.

Kids don't.

Now I was annoyed that I hadn't had a closer look at the confessional before. That would have helped me. I used to observe older children hiding in it. After mass. I think it was some kind of cop and robber game.

Many ecclesiastical objects lose some of their size when dealt with at a less solemn time. She understands them as objects. Not as sanctuaries.

I first put out a dark purple cloth behind the sieve. My eyes slowly got used to the darkness. My throat got drier. Had the time come when I had to pull my note out of my pocket and read it all?

Father Seedorn immediately knew who was in the cabin with him. I first had to think about whether it really was Reverend Seedorn.

Was that actually his voice that I had taken? I was sick.

He could certainly see me, because his eyes were used to this darkness.

55

He could study my facial features, maybe even my pupils. They tell me if I would confess honestly, too.

So I thought.

It was wobbly on this short knee seat. Slowly I pulled the note out of my pocket. What good was he to me now, in this darkness? I hadn't thought of that. I wish I'd inspected the confessional first.

Still, I took the note to hold on to it. But how should I fix it if I should fold my hands during confession? The way we got it explained in communion class? Was it a sin to confess with unfolded hands?

I got more restless. Reverend Seedorn waited for my sins. He was mute. Didn't help me. The palm rest in the confessional was too small to deposit the note there. What was I supposed to do?

I held the paper between my thumb and forefinger, then hastily folded my hands and supported them on the small board. Now I tried to decipher number one. It was still dark. So I had to try to remember.

Stuttering, I said, "I disobeyed."

"To whom?" he asked quickly.

"To my parents," I said.

At first I thought he'd let me list all my sins. But now it became clear that Reverend Seedorn was directing. That made me even more insecure.

What was the next item on the note?

Slowly my pupils got bigger, got used to the darkness. Few words I could recognize on the paper. I wish I'd written it bigger!

"I lied," I said.

"I had a fight with my sister."

I faltered. Sin four. I just thought, "Get it over with in a hurry! Maybe he'll let you out fast. Only give you a few Our Fathers in penance. But not the Way of the Cross, please! I didn't know it by heart. I also didn't like the pictures on the church wall.

I didn't understand them.

In addition, everyone who was with me in the church could see that I had to confess and that I had been imposed a penance by the parish priest, because the Way of the Cross is prayed in front of the pictures.

The Lord's Prayer or the Rosary could be prayed in secret. Maybe even at home.

What was I supposed to do?

I said, "I've done the most outrageous thing. I've tortured flies. I have...," that's all I could get. Because before I could name any more sins, Reverend Seedorn asked questions,

"How many times?"

My jugular swollen. Sweat formed on my forehead. What exposure! What a shame! A shame for my parents, the priest, the class, for the school, for my teacher. For God.

I prayed to God to free me quickly from this predicament - to give me answers.

Yes, did I really pray?

But I was in the house of God!

I confessed my sins to God!

That's what I was here for, and I was supposed to pay. Atonement to get my soul pure. What a shame.

My hands were sweating. The slip of sin, which was tattered anyway by the frequent opening and closing, showed cracks at the creases.

"How many times?" he asked. He expected an answer from me. I had to answer him. Now, at this very moment.

Quietly I said: "Three times," although the meaning of the word was not shamelessly clear to me. Break. It was a crushing pause. I didn't know if I should continue with more sins on my list.

And he said, "A day or a week?"

What was I supposed to say?

I had no sense of time at that moment for days, weeks, months. The question muted me. Again we remained silent in the darkness.

After a while, I said, irritated, "Three times a week." I felt the trap he had set for me. Instinctive.

There was no sound. I hesitated.

Then he said, "What else you got on your note?"

My cramped folded hands came loose a little.

"I stole fruit," I said. "I have..." I read the rest at a faster pace. Then I listened to what the voice on the other side had to say. She didn't say anything to me. Reverend Seedorn began to murmur a little. I tried to understand him. I couldn't. He didn't speak to me either. He looked up, made a sign of the cross in the air, folded his hands, looked down, closed his eyes and then said to me: "Pray the Lord's Prayer ten times and read the Psalm on page 354."

I said nothing, tried to get up, remember what I had to say before I left the confessional. Father Seedorn said, "Praise be to Jesus Christ." To which I automatically replied, "For eternity. Amen." and crucified me.

Slowly I rose, felt the strong tingling of my fallen asleep legs, groped my way out with my hands, grabbed an edge with my left hand, pushed the thick, purple, opaque curtain to the side with my right and was outside faster than I could expect. Through the church windows came a few rays of sunshine, which I first noticed. Afterwards I looked at the benches where a few of my classmates were waiting for the release of the sin.

Silently, I looked for a free bank so as not to obstruct the others. The time in the confessional seemed like an eternity to me.

Did I have to kneel here or was I allowed to sit?

He had said Our Father. Ten times. And what else did he say? I sat down bent. Some psalm. What kind of psalm was that? We didn't discuss that in communion class. A psalm as penance? What about the numbers?

In the hymnbook? In the prayer book? I was thinking, I wanted to collect first. I couldn't think of the number of the psalm. What if I couldn't repent because I couldn't think of the number? Would that be another sin? I didn't know. I didn't know. All I knew was that I had to repent. Right here in the church. I didn't pay any attention to my classmates anymore, I was so busy with myself. I got up, went to the pew in front of the confessional and fetched from there Veronica's prayer book, which she had lent me in the morning. Then I sat down again and leafed through it. Three hundred ... three hundred ... something with three hundred ... there were some fines in it.

Should I take another psalm?

I was insecure. Should I ask Father Seedorn again? But when? He was busy now. I didn't dare.

Our Father, who art in heaven, hallowed be thy name, thy kingdom come, thy will be done, as it is in heaven, on earth ...

Where was the note? Had I lost him? My hand trembled and went into my right pocket. What if someone found him? And talk about it? Lucky you! There he was! I wonder if I'd need it again at the next confession. Would he Bärbel more sins than he does now?

Is it enough to confess once?

How long would that keep me sinless? How long does a confession like that last? Today was Friday. The day after tomorrow should be my first Holy Communion. Day after tomorrow. There was plenty of time. Time to sin.   Then I shouldn't receive the bread. I already had a suit. Dark blue. A dark blue suit. Extra for communion. Matching a bow. And black shoes.

I left the church stunned. Was it raining? Was it windy? Where were my friends?

Without looking around, I went to school.

Next to the pigsty garage was a fallow meadow with molehills. In a corner of the field that could not be seen from the surrounding houses, I searched for the largest of them and distributed the earth with one foot. Then I pulled the confession sheet out of my pocket, tore it into very small

59

pieces and sprinkled the snippets into the hole. Then I piled up the earth again.

First Holy Communion

My mother was waiting for me. She was in the middle of preparing for Sunday. "Well?" she asked and looked at my occupation with me. And as was her way, she immediately involved me in her work. I should get a glass of cherries from the storeroom, she said. Automatically I turned around and went to the pantry next to the kitchen. Mother filled the cake with the following: "I've already ironed your suit..."

I'd worn it before. To try on in the department store. This suit was unfamiliar to me. I never wore a dark blue suit with a bow before. I didn't feel at home in him. And there was a candle, too. Now I put it on again, took the candle in my right hand, tried to hold it straight and carefully walked towards the living room door. The wax stick wobbled. How would I walk with a burning candle? I should have practiced that!

And how would people look at me on this feast day if a breeze suddenly blew out the flame?

They wouldn't let me light the candle for the rehearsal. You were not allowed to do that until Communion Day, in church. A sooty wick makes candles old. He'll look like a burned soul. On a feast day, everything must be new. My classmates would have laughed at me if I had been the only one with a broken candle.

White Sunday. The daily routine was planned. My uncle and aunt were there, my grandparents and some other relatives. How long does a confession like that last? Was I even allowed to talk to people - until communion?

The church bells rang early and woke me. We were all very excited. My clothes were ready and my mother helped me get dressed. She was already festively dressed. My brothers and sisters too. They were waiting at the table in the kitchen.

I got my candle, held it vertically in my right hand and left the house first. No, it still didn't burn. It would only be lit when all the children were in line, my mother said. In the church. We went to the clubhouse. Between the kindergarten, which I had never attended, and the church.

The two buildings were a few metres apart. A narrow path led from here between the church and Sieferts barn to the main road. Coming from this direction, you could see the Wilms restaurant on the other side of the street. Our meeting point was near the entrance to the sacristy, not far from the winding back wall of the church, where men pissed in the dark. The white plaster there showed from hip height down mould-green stains and raised spots that never seemed to age.

The door to the kindergarten was wide open. That allowed me a glimpse inside. No, I didn't want to go in now. What would I be doing there? Some of the children were inside. They talked excitedly with the nuns, who emanated something like a sacred peace.

My mother said that I did not have to go in, I should wait outside, because it would not take long. Some kids were late.

The girls looked beautiful in their white dresses and the decorated sleeves. And a little white bag. Many wore a wreath of hair. And of course the candles.

I was waiting for someone to light mine on fire. I hope my mother had some matches with her!

The group set itself in motion. I was in the back third and took care that the candle was reasonably straight. Just like I practiced in the living room. But now I was no longer alone, but had to look at every step to make sure that I did not step on the heels of the man in front of me.

Even before the church I heard organ music and remembered that Reverend Seedorn had said that we were coming to an ongoing mass. We passed the church doors and walked through the right corridor up to the altar. The faithful sang standing. My excitement didn't allow me to sing along. I had to focus on the candle. My hands were sweating.

Pastor Seedorn wore an unusually embroidered robe that I had never seen on him before. Together with the altar servers he approached us and the group helped each one of us to light his communion candle at the burning Easter candle.

So now it was time! My communion candle was burning. But now I had to wait in a row with the others until all the candles were lit.

I took care that the liquid candle wax did not drip on the hand or suit sleeves on the one hand, and that I held the candle straight on the other hand. I had my misery with this long staff, because a breeze could blow out its flame. The people running back and forth in front of the altar made a lot of wind, I noticed frightened. I hadn't thought of that and no one had told me before.

Could I receive God in me if I celebrated the ceremony without this light? I didn't want to be the only kid who suddenly had no candlelight. What would that look like? Later it would say: "Hihi, look at that one! He ran out of candles!"

After all the candles were lit, we went to a waist-high rack where the altar boys put them. My flame kept burning and - as far as I could see - that of the other children as well.

The girls sat down on the left rows of benches. We boys on the right. Father Seedorn spoke devoutly from the altar to us.

At some point we stepped forward and kneeled down one by one on the communion benches in front of the Altarchor.

"The body of Christ."

"Amen."

And that you would come under my roof. Something flowed through my entire body with enormous power. My knees began to tremble and it ran through my head whether I had confessed everything correctly. How did Father Seedorn say in communion class: "Original sin has every man from birth." And you can't get away from it. No one could be freed from her. Not even by confessing. Not even through many confessions.

So despite confession I was a sinner and should not let God under my roof? Did I have to die now? What happened to me? Would I have all the doubts to confess at the next confession?

As I went back to my seat in the bench, I did not notice how the adults, who had been in the middle of the church all this time, were slowly pouring forward and receiving the holy bread.

I knelt down, as I had observed it in older people before this day. The elbows supported on the front part of the bench, my face placed in the palms of my hands. Only now did I feel that the dry host was sticking to my palate, which was unpleasant for me. I had to create more saliva to get it off him.

The ecclesiastical ceremony was too solemn for me to have the courage to blink between my fingers to see what was going on with the bread. I could hear sounds. Quiet clearing of the throat, occasional draught. My ears didn't fool me. The pastor was still distributing the bread, Jesus Christ. I was sweating, nervous and uncomfortably warm. My new suit captured me. They'd be watching me. God on the inside, the believers on the outside. When did you let me look again? Where was Miss Vormstein, my class teacher and neighbor? Where were Dannbachs? And Ninks?

My father played the organ. Did he have to come down from the gallery and fetch the body of Christ? Then who would represent him? Was he allowed to leave the organ? Where was my mother? My brothers and sisters?

The Hostie had dissolved luckily slowly, so that I could swallow the porridge carefully. Now the time had come to lift my face out of the half shells formed with my hands. A light, cool breath passed through the interspace. Now I felt how wet my face was. I stayed in this position for a moment to let it dry before I was able to find my bank neighbours to the right and left. Tobias didn't kneel anymore. He was sitting on the bench to my right. I should have guessed. For me he was a daredevil who had chewed the body of Christ quickly and then swallowed it. Which is forbidden. The body of Christ must not be chewed. In communion class, Father Seedorn had told us that he was gently dissolved in the mouth and then devoutly swallowed. But never chewed!

Tobias grinned mischievously when he realized that I was watching him from the corner of my eye. During this time I turned my head only slightly, because through a stronger and more jerky movement I would have attracted the attention of the faithful kneeling and sitting behind me. Tobias seemed to suspect that my fear made me act like this.

It was hard for me to hide anything from him. I stayed serious out of reverence for God. I didn't feel like having fun in this place. The priest could see us clearly. Here in the first row. To my left was Jürgen. A stocky boy for his age, with whom I shared a school desk. He had his face still bedded in his hands and prayed.

I now leaned my now round folded hands - flat folding was not usual in our family - on the edge of the bench. Kneeling, I watched the action. The snake of the faithful dissolved in front of the altar choir. After I had the feeling that most of the churchgoers were sitting down, I sat down.

Then altar boys told us to get our candles off the rack. Mine had a paper wreath with blue and yellow lines that I had memorized. Once again we stood in rank and file. With the burning candles in his hand.

Organ music resounded. The faithful rose to the final chant and we were led to the exit by Reverend Seedorn and his altar boys. Again I had to watch out for the flame, which was not allowed to go out in the church under any circumstances.

As soon as we had stepped outside and the first rays of sunshine hit us, most of us started to talk. I asked my mother if I could put the candle out now. She nodded. I blew it and gave it to her.

It was over. A whole year of preparation had now reached its climax.

I breathed a sigh of relief.

Some shook hands. Most parents congratulated their children's friends. This only lasted a short time. We said goodbye quickly and went home.

There we had a festive meal with bratwurst in a dressing gown, woodruff pudding as dessert and the filled cherry cake with cream for the afternoon. But before that my grandfather gave me a songbook with a golden dedication. My grandma gave me a rosary.

My godfather gave me a gold Stowa watch - 17 rubis, anti-shock - with a large second hand - and my godmother gave me an envelope containing fifty marks.

I thanked everyone for that.

After looking at the hymnal, I tried to tie on the first wrist-watch of my life. It was a sensation for me. The clock was already wound, ticked and the time was the same as the current one.

On the following Sundays I always went to Holy Communion. I took great care that I confessed. That my soul was pure and I was not a sinful boy when I let Christ enter. How long was I sinless after a confession?

Was not the thought of original sin a sin?

I kept asking myself these questions. I asked friends - but didn't get any suitable answers.

Did I have to confess immediately when I told the teacher that I had forgotten my homework books at home? But the truth was that I hadn't done the math?

Before the first Holy Communion I was afraid that a teacher would see through me and punish me.

Now the authority of the pastor and God was added to the authority of the teacher. Would Father Seedorn waive my homework sins? What penance would I get? Was Christ allowed under my roof afterwards?

What if I confessed a false sin? Would that be another sin? Who determines what a sin is?

A teacher punished unfinished homework with punishment. That's enough repentance. After the first Holy Communion I was additionally forced to confess this disobedience to the parish priest. The punishment was accompanied by a fine. Only then could I accept the body of Christ.

The village priest was omniscient for me in his spiritual authority. More than a teacher. Because the priest was connected with God because of his profession. With each First Communion, the crowd of people who entrusted him with the most secret and intimate details grew larger. Everyone in the village who had received the body of Christ for the first time belonged from then on to the group of sinners.

Only the priest himself revealed his sins to no one in the village. Could a priest even sin? Wasn't he protected from an early age? Had he not made a general confession forever and ever?

I asked my mother about it. She said that even priests sometimes confess. "But where?" I wanted to know, "there's only him himself!"

"He confesses in another place. With one of his colleagues," she said. I immediately imagined the image of Father Seedorn, dressed in black, waiting in a pew with other sinners to be admitted. Enters the sinner's compartment of the confessional and kneels down in it. However, other believers who were in the church during that time would see that a priest had sinned by entering the confessional. That would call into question his clerical authority.

Anyway, so confessed pastoirs. And indeed. There were days when our priest left the village by bus for an afternoon and came back late in the evening. Then he apparently went to confession.

Did he tell his confessor about the sins he had heard about his sheep? But he wasn't allowed to. That's what we learned in communion class. No pastor was allowed to talk about sins heard. He had to keep her to himself. Only with God did he speak of it in thought. He also spoke to him about repentance. The penance a man had to do.

But how would a priest behave, we asked Father Seedorn in communion class, if a criminal confessed that he had killed someone?

Shouldn't the priest talk about it?

Not even with the police?

"No. Not even with the police," the priest replied. But he could advise the murderer to make a confession, because he would not be able to live with this grave sin, which was a mortal sin. She would torture him and persecute him for the rest of his life.

Thus we learned in class that the sinful person even feels a longing to be punished so that his conscience is relieved. But murderers wouldn't go to heaven. We learned that, too. Moreover, such a difficult deed could not be reversed with a simple penance. While we were talking about it, the priest radiated majesty to me. He was the only person in the village whom I thought every villager from the age of nine had to confide his sins to him. At that thought I became restless, for I felt obliged by the teaching of communion to entrust him with my most intimate secrets.

That made him an omniscient to me. How many children had confessed to him? How many adults? He knew everyone's sins!

When I met the priest in the street, dressed in black, I greeted him politely and shyly and quickly ran past him. At the same time I thought of my sins, which I had to confide to him in my childlike boyishness. What was I left with? Everyone had to go to communion. It was like a law. Everybody did. So do I.

But I only noticed later that there were children and adults in the village who did not go to communion when a friend of my brother visited me. The friend was Lutheran. Protestants did not go to communion. They had confirmation. I didn't know that word. I asked my mother. It was something like that, she said.

Sometimes our Catholic pastor allowed the evangelical faithful to use our church. Only we had a place of worship. We were the ones with the church. The Protestants had none.

The new priest

When I was nine and a half years old, a younger priest came to the village. He was supposed to relieve Reverend Seedorn. I asked my mother why the old pastor left and didn't stay in the village.

He lived here for so many years.

She said he was old and no longer worked as a priest. Besides, he's not from our area, he's from a town. At that time he was assigned to our community by the bishop. Now that he no longer had to work for reasons of age, he had the desire to live in his home town. Reverend Seedorn was the last person I saw working during a Corpus Christi procession.

In the days before, my mother, schoolgirls and women from the village collected grasses and flowers from surrounding meadows. Baskets were carried into the school cellar, the

68

bathtubs there filled with water. The collection should remain fresh for a few days.

In the past, the bathtubs served as public baths, when the village houses had no bathtubs. That must have been a long time ago, because now thick spiders waited half hidden at the spout for prey. And there were no curtains. At federal youth games or football tournaments the tubs were sometimes used.

At the back of the school a part of the quarry stone wall was windowless. Here sawdust was piled up and later distributed. It lay there like a gold carpet. A wooden altar was built, the grasses and blossoms joined to form an ornament.

I had to walk in the procession. But my father didn't. I don't know where he was. The sky was overcast when the train started at the church. I was in the back third. Father Seedorn ran with the monstrance under the canopy. Four strong altar boys carried him and had to take care that Pastor Seedorn was in his midst. We visited several stations, including some wayside shrines in the forest. It started to rain. The priest and his altar boys were not disturbed.

The rain accelerated my walking. I didn't have any rain gear on me. Most other believers don't either. Slowly I approached the canopy. The cloth got wet. And heavier. The altar boys now lifted the rods up with more force. Then I saw that the cloth had formed a depression in the middle. At the canopy bump the water collected, which came through the cloth and destroyed on priest Seedorns bald head to small particles. But he didn't let on and did his job.

On the day I learned that he was leaving, I was uncomfortable because Pastor Seedorn would take away all my sins. He knew all my sins. After all, it was I who entrusted her to him. This obese priest. This man who criticized other men who went to pubs during his sermon and came back before the end of the service. Who complained during the sermon that some men were peeing on the church wall.

He knew more intimate things about me than my parents did. How much did I have to overcome myself to tell him that I had been outrageous? "How many times?" he had wanted to know.

Who could I ask for the meaning of that word?

Insolence?

Who could have explained it to me?

I had in mind that it had to be something that every adult would avoid explaining sensibly. I repeatedly read the Communion Bible - but found nothing about impudence. I didn't want to ask my friends out of shyness. However, I had once picked up on the schoolyard that they were probably forbidden games with the Piephahn.

The change of pastor brought unrest into the village, because everyone was curious about pastor Nahberg, so that numerous questions to the old one fell silent.

From now on the new priest celebrated the masses, which also included the old priest's office. He was much younger than Reverend Seedorn, had no bald head and a cheeky, exploratory gait. He also wore black clothes all the time, but if you faded them away, he would have looked like a taxi driver or bank employee. This would not have been the case with Reverend Seedorn.

A new and unfroter habitus for me. That's why I was less strict in my confession preparations. In the confessional, however, he too could speak with devotion and authoritativeness. That irritated me.

After the First Communion, I reached the age to attend the altar boy lessons. That means my parents sent me there. That's what all the Catholic boys in the village do, they said. And I believed them.

My older brother was an altar boy.

I sometimes saw him in a chasuble during mass. Just not lately. He had got a serious illness that neither we nor the doctors knew how to assess.

Once a week the lessons took place. Pastor Nahberg welcomed us to the first meeting in the sacristy. We should show him that we could kneel without wiggling. We should come back up just as quietly. Some were a bit insecure, but for most the exercise was successful.

We listened with anticipation to what he had to say. During the lessons he was handicapped as priest Seedorn and therefore we asked more questions than before.

But on the subject of impertinence, I didn't want to ask him either.

The new one showed us the interior of the sacristy, led us through the church and let us stay at the altar. Everyone was allowed to stand behind it, just as a priest stood during Mass. I didn't feel as humble behind the altar as I did in the auditorium.

During another altar boy hour Pastor Nahberg had an upright calendar with him. I'd never heard that word before. I couldn't imagine what that meant. The pastor said it meant someone was honest. Especially to yourself. I didn't get that. He said there was a difference whether someone was honest in the eyes of his parents or whether someone knew for himself that he was not thinking or doing anything wrong.

I flipped through this pocket calendar. There were funny drawings in it. Short stories about sacristan. Partly with photos. In one photo, they hung on a bell rope and pulled on it. Five altar boys in robes hanging from a bell rope! They were floating in the air, laughing. And I thought, "Is it okay to laugh in church? This is a holy place! Why are they laughing? That's a sin! You must confess at once! Anyway, before they got the holy bread!

I kept turning the pages. On another page, boys were pictured smoking cigarettes. My neighbor stabbed me in the ribs. I shouldn't look so long, the lessons would soon be over and he wanted to see the calendar as well. I passed it on.

I was never allowed to ring the bells. Only older altar boys were allowed to do that. Like my brother, for example. When he was healthy.

There was one afternoon in the summer when the representative of God let us out of love into his garden, which belonged to the ministry house, after the altar boy lessons. We were allowed to pick strawberries that Father Seedorn would never have allowed us to pick.

Pastor Nahberg dismissed us and went into the house with the hint that we should only choose the ripe berries.

We picked and ate. At least we got the strawberries for free! So we hastily stuffed her inside of us. After some time we had full bellies and went home. It had tasted excellent. Never before had I had the opportunity to eat strawberries fresh from the bushes.

The next morning was school fair. All Catholic children who went to the same school in the village were present. My father was sick, so we didn't hear any organ music. Father Nahberg and the prayer sisters sang songs and drove the faithful through the Mass. Without organ music, it was sad. I was sitting in one of the middle rows.

During the change, we all kneeled, I felt a rumbling in my stomach. Shortly thereafter, gases flowed into my esophagus. Several times I swallowed reflexively, hoping that something would improve. I tried to focus on the worship service. On the devout kneeling during the transformation. Every once in a while, it seemed like my stomach was calming down. Now, while the priest walked water to wine and bread to the body of Christ, to get up and leave the church, I did not dare. I'd never left a service before.

I was too shy. Everyone would have looked at me. The priest first, the nuns, the old mothers who were in the church at every service and knew everyone and everything.

Plus the kids. The big ones and the little ones.

My teachers.

Suddenly I couldn't stick to myself anymore. I spit undigested leftovers of food on my seat and knee bench as well as on my kneeling front man's calves and shoes.

My face got hot and shortly afterwards I felt dizzy. Immediately the faithful in my bank row looked at me.

Those who sat in front turned around in spite of holy transformation. The spotted man in front of me was a disgusting sight.

My anorak was completely smudged. Smudged with escape. I was disgusted, froze and trembled with shame. My kneeling neighbors moved to the side, looked bewildered and irritated at the same time. I didn't want to leave the bank. I remained rigid with fear, because the blessed body of Christ was held up at the altar by Father Nahberg.

A sister came over and whispered at the end of the bank that I should get up, go home and change. She was trying to encourage me. Neighbors joined in quietly. I looked at her questioningly. Who would wipe away the vomit? Would Father Nahberg have to interrupt Mass? What would the man in front do? It was dirty. Did he have to go home too? Was it a sin to break in the house of God?

The vomit stank.

Distraught, I left the bench, turned into the corridor towards the main door, and sneaked out with my head down, without looking at the priest facing the parish. I felt the looks of the believers on me.

Nothing about me I touched.

Even when I was outside, I didn't take my anorak off. I turned into the old way to school.

Here, too, I felt watched. Right and left were houses. That's why I left my head down. But I didn't have any keys! How was I supposed to get into the apartment?

I was thinking of my father's punishing looks. I wonder if he was home. Or a doctor?

He knew it was school fair now. And I'd stay away from her? Luckily, my looks gave me legitimacy to go home. "Just because you're a little sick, you don't stay out of the church."

I was bound to ring the bell. Waiting. After a while, my father opened the door for me. I was surprised he was home. He was alone. His face was bloated. He looked at me. Only now did his yellow eyes strike me. "What happened...?" Take off your clothes. Wash and put on something new," he said. He smelled like booze.

I was afraid at first he'd send me back after I moved. But that would have been an even greater embarrassment for me: to go back to the current mass after the change and pretend that nothing had happened. Besides, I didn't know if my vomit was still on the benches. I didn't want to go back. I was miserable and I didn't know if there was any supplies left.

I took off my clothes, washed myself and put on something fresh. I was freezing. I was afraid my father would say, "So, now you've washed and changed. Now go to school."

I felt he was going to send me. That's why I said I didn't feel well and wanted to stay home. I was weak. He didn't seem to notice my deep shame.

That day, I couldn't have focused on the lessons. I didn't know if it would go the next day because I was afraid of being teased by my classmates. But this day off was of no use to me in escaping their hostility. On the following school day, they said it was "the smell of the great wide world."

The scent of the great wide world.

If only it had been the weekend in between. How much I wished for that. Children do not escape children. At the most, if you change your place of residence.

I was ashamed of Miss Vormstein too.

During the big break she took me aside and quietly told me to leave the church early the next time I felt something like this. How can you puke in church? What blasphemy!

Sometimes the sentence about the scent of the big wide world made the rounds. I couldn't eat strawberries anymore. No one knew if it was that or not. It was just a hunch from my parents.

The forbidden tree

On my way home I crossed the narrow asphalt road between the church and the school. At the level of the footbridge, which led across the stream near the parsonage, I discovered ripe hazelnuts on the tree for the first time. I stopped on the little bridge and looked at the fruits with fascination.

I knew hazelnuts from the Christmas plate. They were brown. These were green and had leaves. It was not clear to me whether the hazelnuts were roasted from the Christmas plate and only then became edible. Or if I could eat those nuts from the tree. If they were ripe enough. I was thinking of the strawberries from that time.

Some hazelnuts hung across the property. Someone once told me that you could take the fruit that hung over a piece of land. That's not stealing.

I climbed the hip-high stone wall of the bridge to take a close look at the hazelnuts. When I was upstairs, I noticed that the tree was standing on the parsonage grounds. Then I remembered that Reverend Nahberg could be home and see me.

The seventh commandment is: Thou shalt not steal!

Maybe that wasn't true for those fruits that crossed the property line?

I sought shelter behind leaves and branches. Since the tree stood in the extended axis of the house corner, it would have been difficult for Father Nahberg to discover me. Leaning out of the window I would have seen him and immediately escaped. His housekeeper wasn't there. I saw her walking towards the cemetery before.

With Reverend Seedorn I would never have allowed myself to climb the stone wall and look at hazelnuts. Pastor Nahberg, however, seemed to have more understanding because he had us pick strawberries in his garden.

While I thought about the Ten Commandments, I looked at the hazelnuts. Touched a fruit and wondered if it could be eaten.

Only now did it occur to me that Pastor Nahberg could come out of the house. Thanks to the hedge cover I was protected, and he could only catch me after leaving the property.

But maybe he was resting. From the exhausting church work.

My desire to pick and taste hazelnuts increased. I took a branch in one hand and touched a hazelnut with the other. Was she ripe? God had already punished me once with unripe fruits, although she gave us His representative. Maybe God wanted to punish me then? Had I confessed properly before the strawberry dinner? Or made a mistake confessing? Was I punished for that?

I was thinking of my penance.

The hazelnut branch towered over the fence and bridge railings. I pulled three hazelnuts from the branch with one hand and let go of it.

Now I wanted to jump off the wall. At that moment Father Nahberg came out of the sacristy and saw me. I quickly threw the hazelnuts into the stream and jumped off the stone wall. I hope the nuts went down. But it was too late. He must have been watching me for a moment. As if rooted, I stopped. I didn't dare escape. He came closer to a quick step.

"I just wanted to take a look," I said distraught. "I didn't take anything."

"Thou shalt not steal! is the seventh commandment," he said.

I was very ashamed and looked to the ground.

"Go home now."

I've been dealing with this incident for a long time. Especially if I should confess him to Reverend Nahberg. But why? I wouldn't have to confess that to him. He'd been watching me. They only confessed sins the priest hadn't seen.

Nevertheless, I confessed to him that week that I stole hazelnuts from his garden.

Bärbel

I played with her in the little sawdust hollow. It had no stone or wood border and was located to the side of the school, a few metres from the flight of steps. Bärbel was in my class. I liked her.

She conveyed something quiet that I liked. We were supposed to meet this afternoon at the Kuhle. It was the first time I met a girl outside class - to play.

I was very lucky she got permission from her mother to see me. It was a warm early autumn day and we enjoyed the indivisible joy. None of our common friends bothered us and that was a good thing. We didn't think to do anything with our playmates.

We both squatted in the sawdust and told each other something, while we formed the sawdust with buckets, shovels and moulds.

I had brought water from the kitchen so that we could also use it to let small trickles flow.

Bärbel was a lively girl with blue eyes. Her facial features were of delicate form, without aggressive notches. I enjoyed their existence and wished this day would never end. I forgot all about time.

When my mother called for the first time, I wanted the sawdust cooler to be somewhere else.

On the second call, I pretended not to hear it. I sat with my back to the house, which made it easier to overhear. My mother shouted louder, "Can you hear me?" Bärbel, who sat facing the house, said that my mother was at the window and wanted something from me. Slowly, holding a mould in my hand, I turned around. My mother looked out of the toilet window on the first floor.

"You have to come up soon," she said. "You can play for five minutes, but then you come up!"

"What a bummer!" I said to Bärbel. "And we're playing so beautifully."

"Yes!" she said in a sad voice and lowered her eyes, "I would also like to play with you longer."

I forgot the call, and we kept playing.

Suddenly I drove together: "You come up right now," my mother shouted loudly and angrily.

Bärbel looked at me confused. She was twitching and began to tremble like me. Maybe she felt my restlessness, because her eyes seemed to ask me the questions: "Are you going immediately? Must we finish our beautiful game now?"

Seconds passed.

"Please come at once," it echoed behind me.

"You can still play tomorrow."

I got up, looked at the door, then I looked up. I saw my mother, walked up the stairs, stood under the window to be closer to her and asked if I could stay a few more minutes.

We played so beautifully and Father wasn't here for dinner yet. "It'll be dark soon," she said, "and Bärbel has to go too!"

"But she doesn't live far from here," I replied. "She's quick to get home."

"No, you're coming up right now!" she said energetically.

78

I went back to the sawdust den, where Bärbel waited patiently for me and sat down with her. Back to school. Bärbel's closeness gave me strength. It wasn't long before I heard my mother's extremely aggressive voice. She seemed closer now, lower now. I trembled again because something strange for me resonated in her voice.

I didn't know what to do. I felt very comfortable near Bärbel. She was the first girl I ever played alone with. Now I regretted being this close to school with her.

Bärbel had jumped up and looked at the front door. Their restlessness frightened me. I jumped up nervously and turned around.

We both saw my mother disappear into the entrance. Now I had no choice, I had to go to the door. I hastily said goodbye to Bärbel, went to the front door and thought that my girlfriend certainly had a gentler courage.

With a dull feeling I reached the flight of stairs and stopped frozen in front of the house when I discovered my mother in the doorway. I wasn't expecting that. Why did she do that? I had followed her request. Why was she waiting in the doorway now? She'd never done that before.

With her left hand she held the door to be opened inwards. I didn't see the right one. I saw her head and part of her trunk in the doorway.

"You come up right now!" she repeated in a sharp voice. Her eyes showed lifeless cold. Something's wrong, I thought. Did I do something bad? Why was she waiting for me here?

I was insecure, with small steps I walked towards the door. My mother's rigid gaze held me prisoner.

She was very excited.

I had to climb five stone steps. Then there was a small one that was right in front of the entrance. My mother didn't leave. So I couldn't get through the entrance. There wasn't enough room. Now she took a step back, but held the door with her left hand. I still haven't seen your right hand. I was creepy. I did not know such an experience. What did she want with me? Her prey eyes wouldn't let me go.

"I'm here and I'm going up," I said quietly - and I looked down.
Now she opened the door another inch of her body width. I passed the last step, then the door. When I was in the stairwell, my mother slammed the door into the lock with tremendous force. She lifted her right arm at lightning speed, holding our blue bamboo cane in her hand. Quickly my right hand shot upwards to defend myself. I ducked down at the same time and quickly reached the first step with my right foot. The stick crashed on my back. Once, twice. The third shot missed my body and I ran up the stairs faster than ever before.
My mother screamed after me. She got angrier because I had escaped her, but she seemed sure she could punish me more upstairs in the apartment. Our home didn't have an escape route. All the classrooms, the cellar and the large roof shelves were locked at this time of day. You can't escape a mother like that. We both knew that, because her upbringing included physical punishment.
With my right hand I grabbed the curvature of the handrail, pulled myself to the next staircase with a strong jerk and arrived at the apartment. Fortunately, the apartment door was open. Now I screamed, felt surrounded, didn't know where to go. At first I walked straight through the long corridor into the kitchen where my sisters and brother sat at the table. Wordlessly, I touched an arm while running, pleading for help, knowing at the same time that it was impossible to escape our mother's punishment.
My mother quickly followed me around the round kitchen table. She screamed at me to come to her immediately and not make any fuss. It just makes things worse. I reached the kitchen door that she had locked, ripped it open with all my might, saw the open living room door on the right, consi-

dered for a moment whether I should flee through the apartment door, but turned into the living room for fear of more severe punishment and slammed the door shut. Then I rushed, rolled under the round living room table, whimpering like a dog and waiting for the punishment to be given quickly.

My mother was quick on the spot.

She closed the door. Now we were alone.

Nobody would help me.

She grabbed one of my arms, pulled me out from under the table and drove me in with tremendous power. I rolled back and forth crying, tried to tear myself free, to escape her again, but she gave me no chance. As she struck, she repeated the words from the beginning: "I have told you a thousand times to come up, you naughty child. Why don't you obey when I tell you something?"

I avoided eye contact with her, let my hand fall to the ground, covered my face with it sobbing and curved myself full of pain on the floor.

Crying, I crawled to the door - she had long since left. How long did it take? I didn't know. I didn't know.

Slowly I opened the door and walked through the kitchen, where my siblings were still sitting, into my room. There was nothing to eat for me.

I was ashamed and went to bed after putting on my pyjamas. I kept crying. How long, I don't remember.

I felt my mother's jealousy towards Bärbel. It wasn't important to her that I get home on time. It was more important to her that I didn't see Bärbel anymore. I resented my mother for that.

This pain stabbed deep into my soul and I didn't know if I would ever again be allowed to play with a girl in a sawdust box. In the following days I often felt observed by my mother. Even if she was not present or could see me, how and with whom I was playing, she was there in my mind and had the ability to determine my actions. From this time on I met Bärbel very distanced. Probably. Probably knew why. We didn't talk about it. It would have been pointless.

Up to my adulthood I dreamed of this punishment experience in different variations again and again. On the morning of December 8, 1990, after another nightmare, I wrote this letter:

Dear parents
your life building is cold
an icy wind is blowing through the windows
that's been passing by clattering doors
makes its way through every floor

He sweeps through rooms without furniture
glides past faded wallpaper
and swirled around in the attic
the dust of buried longing for love

Mother? You say it's about love? What kind of love? I'm telling you, a facade love. Visible to all from the outside, "Look here, you people, I love my husband, that is why I save him from the flight of life with the full commitment of the feelings of my children". I don't care that I'm abusing my children with it. I trample on their souls. They're still so small and tender. But I'm ignoring that. I have only one goal: to save my husband from the deadly alcoholism that I worshiped him for to return to me. Because he found love and affection in another woman. For seven years. 2555 days and nights.
It takes strength. You said God gave you this power? By praying? With such prayers: "Lord, let Franz be sick, so that

I can nurse him and he loves me again?" What a price. God's price!
I get sick of so much hypocrisy. Do you know when my father died for me? When he started drinking and he 'asked' me to get beer and booze for him in the pub. Wagenbachs. In the evening I had to sneak past between the church, kindergarten and Sieferts barn. Where our meeting place for the first Holy Communion was. Next door - in the church - the priests mentioned Sanctus Spiritus.
I am convinced that addicted spirits cloud the way to God and agree with C. G. Jung: Spiritus contra Spiritum.
Remember that? I should always go through the side door. So no one would see me. But all the guests recognized me immediately. They made stupid remarks. About your husband.
How I was ashamed.
I made sure that the bottles didn't beat each other when I walked. You know that sound of empty beer bottles when you clink when you walk? And the dull sound of full bottles?
I shamefacedly handed the money to the landlord and was on my way back to school. That big black bunker of emptiness. I wonder where he was now. With Miss Grewen? I couldn't think of anything like that because you were man and wife. Catholic wedding. Always together. Till death do you part.
I put beer and booze in the closet. Remember that? In the drawer of the big living room closet. The compartment that always smelled so different after opening than the other compartments.
The lower ones smell of Sunday table linen, freshly rinsed Rosenthal porcelain and cut glasses.
The drawers released the aroma of cleaned silver cutlery, cloth napkins and guest chocolates. Only the right compartment, this right cabinet compartment, with the swing door, smelled like alcohol. Remember that? Some bottle of

83

blackbird fields had formed a red wreath on the bottom of the cabinet board. I never could figure that out. Every time I opened the drawer, the bottles stood upright in it. And corks were stuck in their necks. Even though they weren't full anymore, these bottles. How should the bottom of the bottle form a wreath of wine? Were all these bottles leaking downstairs?

The new village school

I saw my father less and less. In addition to his work as headmaster, teacher, organist, mentor and carnival entertainer, he was involved in the planning and construction of the new school, which was to become the secondery general school. He got sicker. Nevertheless, he made a speech. The whole village was on its feet. Besides teachers and pupils, the school council, the mayor, the architect, the priest, the doctor, important people who celebrated the completion of this village building project and its inauguration met in winter.

The new school building looked different from the old one. Elongated and box-shaped. With a monopitch roof, big windows. Above the auditorium was my father's principal's room and the teachers' room, whose façade was covered with brown wood. The rest of the front was painted white.

The old school building was grey, with smaller windows and a saddle roof made of natural slate. It looked more like a house on the outside. The new schoolyard was also different: made of grey, ugly asphalt.

Even weeds couldn't get through. It was also rectangular and lay in front of the school building. In some places there were fixed wastebaskets made of zinc sheet metal, but no angle into which one could have crawled away in order not to be seen by the break supervisor. With the old schoolyard

84

with small gravel stones it was different. It was bigger and offered enough hiding places, because the school was in its middle. It was possible to walk around the building during breaks, to hide behind the old fire engine house or the pigsty garage. You couldn't be seen by the teacher.

The break supervisors were therefore overwhelmed with the old schoolyard.

I learned that the auditorium was used by students to take a break in bad weather and let off steam. That was not possible in the old school, which was now to become primary school. There one remained then in the classes to sit.

The floor in the new school building was shining like glass. He looked like marble. The walls of the auditorium were decorated with thick, polished pine boards instead of pictures or murals. That seemed strange to me.

My father said during his inauguration speech that these woods were symbolic of the surroundings. The village was surrounded by pine forests and there were many sawmills in the surrounding valleys.

I was standing among my classmates. My father briefly set a tone on a brightly coloured piano and we began to sing. No, I think he accompanied us on this little piano and conducted with one hand. Where was my mother? I had no idea.

It's a children's piano, I thought, because it wasn't as high as our dark family piano.

That's why the school piano wasn't a piano for me.

My father later said that it was just as much a piano as ours, only smaller and therefore lighter. The most important exception is that it has fewer keys - almost an octave less. It is more handy and therefore easier to roll. This is ideal for school celebrations or school carnivals. Besides, it's cheaper. However, old and larger pianos sound fuller. You'd have more volume.

What we sang? Rehearsed songs like Good Moon, you walk so quietly.

The choir sang, my father played. It must have been several songs. Maybe five. I can't remember. Then the group disbanded. After the celebration, visitors were able to view the classrooms.

Some students from higher classes found a new school less interesting, I heard. They were happy to finally finish school and earn money in a profession.

We went through school. A long, narrow corridor, which was not very bright because small windows were walled in here, adjoined the auditorium. There were many doors in the corridor, in between metal coat hooks on the walls, which I noticed immediately because they were all attached upside down. The curves of the hooks arched into the corridor. Their openings pointed to the wall. I wondered and thought a mistake had been made. How to mount clothes hooks upside down? I wanted to ask someone, but I didn't dare, because the school was only inaugurated today. She was new. Maybe you weren't allowed to ask that now?

Nevertheless, this occupied me so much that I couldn't think clearly. I had to find my father who could give me that answer. Because he had helped build the school. He was partly responsible for that. I'm sure he knew the right answer. I didn't want to ask another teacher. He probably would have thought me to be simple or: How can one deal with wrongly mounted coat hooks?

I touched one of these hooks and wondered if my jacket would stick to it. I wondered if I could even twist my fingers so that the loop of the jacket fitted on the hook. I didn't want to try it now. That would have been embarrassing for me, because pupils, teachers, the mayor, the priest and other authorities could have observed me.

All the hooks were upside down. On all hook rows. Who could I ask? I didn't see my father. I'm sure he was very busy and would feel disturbed if I tried to ask him. Besides, he was sick. I needed courage to talk to someone else. Teachers who taught me could not do it. To give me the nakedness as the main teacher's son to address this question to them embarrassed me. For the same reason, I didn't want to ask classmates.

I got queasy. I needed an immediate answer to the hook problem. I was wandering the corridor. Most of the guests had passed the rows of hooks. If I didn't address anyone right now, my chance would have passed. There wouldn't be any people here later. You'd have other thoughts on your mind than the shoe initiation. That's why no one would take their time on the way back.

I followed the group. A few adults stood at a class door and looked into the room: "...and maybe they saw the hooks in the corridor...?!" one man said, "...we had to mount them the wrong way round because of a building regulation. The kids get hurt very quickly if they don't. "If they were to romp and wobble in the corridor, they wouldn't break their heads."

So that's why. I quickly took a few steps back and tested this possible incident: I stood near a hook and saw how it could work. It made no sense to me not to be able to hurt myself. Because the hooks were made of hard metal.

If a child were to stumble or be pushed, it could still be seriously injured.

With these thoughts I went back and came across my class-mates who entered a classroom with Miss Vormstein.

After we entered, she said we should find our seats at the new tables and chairs. And then she said how nice it would be to teach in a new school. Above all, that from now on every class has its own classroom.

I got used to the new environment and to the use of the objects in this school very slowly. We were temporarily in the new school with the fourth grade until the old one was converted into a primary school. From then on, the fourth should be back in the old house. But separate from the third.

The windows in the new building were directly opposite the door. We all sat along the row of windows and had a view of the new schoolyard.

The new school building was not as practical as the old one. If you sat in the ground floor classes and walked along the building with other students whose classes began later or were finished earlier, you could see them. And they could look in and fax when the teacher had instantly turned to the blackboard.

That distracted me. In the old school, the windows were higher. There were also a few bushes and shrubs in front of it. At the new school it was forbidden to knock on the outside of the windows under penalty.

I was particularly disturbed by those windows. Especially when you only had a second or third lesson or - and that was much more important - when you were late. Then, namely, began to run the gauntlet already outside school. Teachers and students had long since noticed that you were late.

It also made me feel guilty because I saw classmates learn and I didn't learn.

Some children were chosen more or less voluntarily to take over a certain class service. For example, as class president. Some were responsible for collecting the milk and cocoa money, others for maintaining the school books, which were no longer in the vicarage. I signed up to get a map. It took a long time until we needed one in class.

When we had geography lessons with Fräulein Vormstein, she unexpectedly gave me her key and sent me with Jürgen to the map room. So far I had not done such services, neither had my classmate, and always thought I had time during the break - or before class - to get the cards out of the card room and hang them up in class. Especially since we weren't familiar with the map room. Now Miss Vormstein challenged us in the middle of class. We were under time pressure because we didn't know if we would find the right card before the end of the lesson. Perhaps the teacher believed that as the main teacher's son I was more aware of the school interior than other pupils. We did not live in the new school, but my father had a master key which he would never have entrusted to me.

Slowly we unlocked the new door security lock, opened the door, looked for the light switch and had to wait a while after taking the picture until it was light. Because in the new school there were neon tubes that took a while to light up. From the old school we only knew spherical frosted glass lamps hanging from the ceilings on long chrome rods. If you operated their switches, you could immediately see something.

It smelled of paint and glue in this windowless room that I had imagined to be bigger. My classmate and I had to find our way.

The map was found after some search time. That's why we went in pairs, so that we could find them faster and so that one of them - in case the other should get sick - could carry out the card collection service on his own. It was an old map. At first I thought she was new, too, because of the new school. But I was disappointed that she was old. Some others, too. The old cards didn't match this new school.

We went back to the class where our classmates and teachers were sitting and waiting for us. The map was hung under the watchful eye of the others. We had to quickly familiarize ourselves with the functionality of the new metal card stand. In the old school there were wooden stands. I regretted not having hung up a card unobserved with the new stand before.

After the map hung, Miss Vormstein pointed to it. But only once. That disappointed me, because the fetching was out of proportion to the showing.

The school bell rang and my classmates rushed out.

I wanted to run along, but then Miss Vormstein reminded me that I had map service and had to make sure that the map was back in its place. And, above all, that the door of the card room was correctly locked again.

I reluctantly did my duty and was annoyed that the time went by from the break.

Hahn

He was my class teacher in fifth grade. Mr. Hahn taught mathematics and was about as old as my father.

One school day I hadn't thought about completing the house tasks. There were a few tasks to be solved from the book. In addition, the once-three-ten should be memorized. This only occurred to me when the teacher was already in class and had asked one of my classmates. Now there was no turning back, I thought. It could be highly-then that he overlooks me and only tests those who were sitting in the front rows. He went through the central aisle to the rear bench rows and took samples.

As soon as he noticed that someone could do it fluently, he chose another student. As a classmate spoke, teacher Hahn approached my table more and more. Always one ear turned to the pupil who was just about to recite the parcel. During his search, Mr. Hahn made special fun of approaching a student with the intention of calling him immediately, but then he gave the name of a student who was not in his field of vision. That was his pedagogical idiosyncrasy.

As well as his special punishment: some pupils who had not done their homework had to get up in the classroom. Teacher Hahn grabbed the back of his head and under his chin with his strong hands and lifted the student up so that his feet dangled in the air. When I first saw this, I thought the neck could break.

He came up to me, looked at me with concentration, so that I thought: now he is taking Ursula, because she is behind him.

But when teacher Hahn looked at me longer and nodded benevolently at me, he seemed to give me courage.

Meanwhile I had tried to listen carefully while my class-mates recited the one-time thirteen. In this way I wanted to learn along with them, so that if I was asked to, I could at least effortlessly get to five.

Now what? Now I was irritated and remembered Fräu¬lein Vormstein, who had not left me alone. It's an embarrassing situation. And then there was a teacher who was not only my father's deputy, but also his double-headed partner. At the next game meeting at Gasthof Wilms he would certainly tell him what a bad student I was.

"And what about you?" teacher Hahn asked me.

My classmates looked over at us expectantly. I got up, start-led, and said, "Once thirteen is thirteen." He looked at me. His facial expressions indicated that any I-Male could also say that. "Twice thirteen is..." I needed time to think. I tried to add quickly. But I couldn't. What was I left with? He immediately realized that I had to think long and hard.

I hoped he thought I could do the one-time thirteen, but was now too shy to express myself in front of the class. Because I was known as a quiet student. Not as one of those raving ones who had to play their way into the foreground all the time. I looked into emptiness, while teacher Hahn stood next to me and looked towards the blackboard.

Behind his back he impatiently slapped his hands against each other and waited for an answer.

I'm just holding up the whole class, I thought. The ordeal will soon be over at the court.

Tell him to give me a five and that's it.

While I was thinking that, I was waiting for a soft shout from my class. My neighbour could certainly have given the answers, but teacher Hahn stood next to me so that nothing would be told to me.

Teachers are doing well, I thought, they don't have to learn all this stuff anymore and don't have to be humiliated in front of all their classmates.

Did I hear you right? He himself gave me the answers? Suddenly I knew the results. He whispered it to me. And I started repeating them out loud. That was worse for me than to remain silent, because the solutions did not come from me. This teacher was obviously standing next to me to help me. Quiet, but audible to those sitting around, he called the results.

At that moment, we were sort of a sworn community. But wouldn't this situation make it clear to my classmates that he was good friends with my father? Wasn't what he did considered corrupt? The people sitting behind me couldn't have noticed our supposed agreement, but they must have realized what a disgrace it was for me.

This teacher put me in a more uncomfortable position than she already was. Nothing would have been more honest than to make me look like a fool and ask another student.

Now I was forced to listen to him and repeat everything like an automaton. Until a new thought came to my mind: What if he wanted to put me to a hard test, told me wrong results, which I repeat in my good faith, and through his mockery and that of the class, would come to me? Because in this situation I was not able to verify the results before I how-recovered them. Could I trust him or not? I didn't know what to do. It was more shameful than with Fräulein Vormstein, because I was in a higher class and was older.

I was unable to verify these results accurately. I had to turn myself over to him. I didn't stand a chance. Bent, I stood on the tabletop on which I rest my hands. How could a few seconds mean such eternity?

At 130 the procedure was over. Disappointed, he went to the front desk and asked us to open the mathematics book. I sat down slowly and thought of nothing for a moment. I didn't want to look at my neighbors. Everything was so far away. The school, the houses, my parents.

Had teacher Hahn whispered the results to me because my father was his superior or because I was to be transferred to grammar school? Some teachers had spoken out in favour of the change. It was the time when my father was in hospital and had to be represented as headmaster. From Teacher Hahn. And it was the time when my mother had to get a driver's license so we could visit my father.

The Gymnasium

With other children from the village, the day began with boarding an old bus that brought us to Kürstadt. The journey took some time and led over mountains. This bus ride was a pleasure at first, but later it became a painful torture. It began with the bus driver demanding a new ticket every month when boarding the bus.

I bought the monthly tickets in the village drugstore Sehrlaub. Here I sometimes bought erasers and ink cartridges for myself, because meanwhile I had a modern cartridge fountain pen.

In this drugstore, which was close to the post office, I also bought Bommerlunder for my father.

Back then.

The drugstore owner never looked his customers in the eye, but on their foreheads. That always made me embarrassed. He wrapped the bottle in grey paper so that you wouldn't see the label after I left the store. But my father didn't need the liquor anymore, because he said he wanted to die.

One always had to pay attention to the validity of the monthly ticket and could not lose it, otherwise one would not have been able to ride along.

Every morning we students stood at the bus stop and waited for the bus. Sometimes a blue one came, sometimes a red one. Blue or red with wide white stripes. The bus driver was big. It struck me because there weren't many great people in the village. His name was Konrad Sternemann. And was called Sternemanns Konrad. He was taciturn and only sometimes said good morning. But that could only be right for us, for what should we have talked to him about?

When we boarded, we had to show our monthly season tickets. Mr. Sternemann just nodded.

My brother had given me a used protective cover for the ticket so that it wouldn't break. But the protective cover got cracks and I repaired it with self-adhesive clear strips. When I showed my ticket the following day and wanted to pass by the driver's seat, Mr Sternemann stopped me and said that he could not recognize the ticket - I should buy a new plastic cover. Then I pulled the card out of the cellophane and showed it to him.

Most of the time we went to our regular places and looked out of the window. Fortunately, the bus tour began in our village, so that we always had a large selection of free seats.

The bus stopped in other places and more children boarded, who also went to high school. In the beginning you didn't know any of them. It wasn't until you got to know each other that you made friends, if you liked it. If we were lucky, the bus driver took us to the school above a mountain. But if it was ever too much work for him, we had to get off at the city border and walk the long way. Of course we had to hurry, because we didn't have much time until the beginning of the lessons. The children of rich parents had an additional bus ticket. They could use them for one of the city buses and have them brought to the school gate.

The headmaster of the school was named Mielmann and was about sixty years old - with a conspicuous, bulbous nose. He was fat, had a very dark voice and thus radiated an enormous authority. When he screamed, he screamed very loudly. That's what we were all afraid of.

Our class was in the attic and the room had double wooden windows. I hadn't seen that before.

A handful of classmates from the village school were in my new class as well as other children I didn't know. That's why I sat next to my friend Tobias. In our village school I had not sat next to him, but now a feeling of loss gripped me amidst all these strange and noisy children, so I preferred to sit next to a well-known boy. Klaus and Jürgen were accommodated in a parallel class.

During the break we saw them in the schoolyard, but they were already playing with their new classmates. It was an unfamiliar feeling.

So many unknown children - some almost grown up.

And unknown teachers. My former school wasn't as big as this one. Little by little I could remember the names of my new teachers. We had more fans.

There was a Miss Fencing. An old gray-haired woman who taught us English. Obviously she was never married, because she - like teacher Vormstein - also let herself be approached by Fräulein. I was sitting in the second row of the bench and she had asked me to read something. I was so nervous, I moved my knees under the bench. She saw that and told me not to do it. It's driving her crazy.

Consequently, I was forced to watch my knees while reading. I couldn't make friends with this woman. She was too unfriendly for that. And too strict.

Another teacher was named Nock. A great name for a teacher, I thought! When I saw him, he always wore a blue tracksuit from Adidas. With the three white stripes. The pedagogue carried a ball under his left arm, a silver pipe on a ribbon around his neck and in his right hand his key ring. He was also dressed in an Adidas sports shirt and matching shoes from the same manufacturer. I never saw him in civilian clothes.

That's why he reminded me of my encounters with the village priests.

If I'd met Mr. Nock in civilian clothes, I certainly wouldn't have recognized him.

I was looking forward to his gym class as long as it was about athletics. In athletics I was good to very good. It's always been great fun for me. On the cinder track. After all, I almost won an honorary certificate at the Federal Youth Games in our village once. I was only five points short. Mr. Nock made many runs with us. I didn't know that before. You've been exhausting. But they are good for the condition, he often said.

I didn't like swimming. At first, we always had to walk very far to the outdoor pool. And secondly, this teacher was very strict with us. We actually had to be able to do everything.

Not only breaststroke, but also crawling, diving and of course jumping off the tower.

I couldn't swim and envied those who could. As a young child, I almost drowned. I haven't liked swimming pools since. But Christine, who came to school on a different bus than I did, could swim well.

In winter my mother, Marlene and I drove by car on the way back from the hospital to Bromberg. When we arrived in the village, the shops were still open, but it was dark. We bought groceries and an alarm clock.

For my father.

At the hospital.

I kept thinking about Christine, who lived here in this beautiful place, and wished that she would come out of any house and I would meet her. But what should I say then?

And what if she wasn't alone, but with her parents? It was dark. She wouldn't dare go out on the street alone.

I fell in love with Christine. She had a graceful, tender face and beautiful blonde, curly hair. I never told her I was so close because I was afraid. She was a good student. In class, I kept looking at her from the row of windows. She was sitting in the wall row. We were separated by iron-braced desks that had inkwell depressions.

Christine, I don't think you've paid any attention to me. You just kept looking at Bernd, who could already read the paper. And who lived in the same village as me. Too bad. But I lacked the courage to speak to you, because my mother had already beaten me once over a girl.

There were courageous people in the class who seemingly jumped without fear from the ten meter tower. They got an A for that proof of courage.

I had a hard time swimming. It took me a long time to realize that you can't go down without a plastic buoyancy aid. You could borrow them at the swimming pool. It looked like a small gothic church window and had handles. So I practiced under supervision first in the non-swimmer pool. Later in the swimming pool. Along with others who couldn't swim. I envied students who could swim because they were allowed to swim in the deep pool without teacher supervision. I liked that.

In addition, Mr. Nock made Kneipp baths with us during forest runs. In the near surroundings of Kürstadt there were pools. Most of the time we first walked through the forest for a while and then kneippted in the basins. The water was always very cold.

I remember one victory: once again we were on our way back to school after a forest run. Near the jump-jump there was a steep slope. Teacher Nock spontaneously said that we should all walk up vertically until we reached a hiking trail that passed above. Whoever's top first should be victorious. With a whistle in his silver whistle he gave the starting signal. We started running. To my right and to my left the classmates flew up the mountain. I ran with him. After a few meters, I had pudding calves. I wanted to give up. But then I saw that I was in the front position. I immediately pulled myself together and walked on. I won. The others had given up or were beaten. At the top, I threw my arms in the air. What a triumph! Finally I could shine, but I also had the longest way back to the group.

Mr. Mossner was our class teacher. He was a student assessor. What was that supposed to be? An assessor? I was told at home that this was a teacher who still had to take a final exam.

He taught us German.

Mr Weber, whom my brother already knew, taught us drawing because he attended the same school as I did for several years. But when I was in the sexta, my brother wasn't in school anymore. He was in hospital again for several months and we visited him. My mother said he had chronic diarrhea. This should come from the many sweets that he had always bought at the little shops in the city. That was true. My brother always had candy, liquorice or gum with him.

Mr Weber lived in the same village as us and measured the snow depth there in winter. He used to be an art teacher, We should paint a landscape once. I couldn't think of anything suitable. That's how I first designed a tree. During the lesson Mr Weber went through the bank series. Then he stopped at my bench and looked at my sketch: "I don't understand," he said, "are the trees in Kleinenbach thinner at the bottom than at the top?

It annoyed me that he had come to me early, because I was not yet finished painting. So he exposed me to the mockery of my classmates. Then I spasmodically tried to make the tree thicker with paint at the bottom. But that didn't look like it at all.

I told my brother at the hospital. "Don't worry about it," he said, "next time it'll be better."
My brother once drew a fantastic skier on a slope behind which a snowball shaped avalanche rolls. The skier flees from the avalanche. My brother was a good draughtsman.

I had to repeat the sexta because my grades were bad. Christine's been transferred. And friends from my village. Bernd, Tobias, Sabine...
It was a lonely time for me because I had disappointed my parents. They wanted me to be a doctor. Just like my four cousins. "If you can't become a doctor, then you can become a teacher, but you have to do your Abitur," they said.
But I didn't know what I wanted to be.
During the big holidays we visited my father more often in the hospital. He got worse. And I thought the reason was that I wasn't transferred like my classmates.
The new school year began. This time the class teacher's name was Diel and he was also a study assessor. I think I kept the other teachers.
Mr. Diel wrote several names on the blackboard, which were mentioned to him by classmates, concerning the election of the class spokesman and his deputy. Someone must have called my name, because he was suddenly on the table. That made me mute - I didn't want to - but was too shy to say anything against it. Silently I hoped that no one would choose me, as there were more names on the blackboard.
Then we had to cast our votes on scraps of paper. The notes were collected and counted. Strokes were made behind the names. Whoever gets the most strokes should become class president. I didn't choose myself. Behind Gerhardt's name were most of the stick packs, followed by my name. Mr. Diel asked us if we would accept the election.
Gerhardt said, "Yes." It went too fast for me. But since my name was on the blackboard and there were more strokes

behind it than on the other candidates, I thought I couldn't refuse the election. A no didn't come from my lips. Without knowing what a deputy would do, I nodded.

I didn't like the election, I didn't like my office.

In the current school year, the class teacher asked who was in favour of another deputy being elected. Most of them raised their arms. So do I.

The year passed. The grades got better. Sometimes I would buy PEZ sweets on the way back from the city. At the vending machine near the bus stop. As I waited for the bus, I wondered if my father would still be alive if I came home. I thought I was to blame for his illness because I bought him beer and booze. I also wondered if I should confess my actions, because my father was terminally ill. Was I a murderer?

Would I go to heaven? Had I committed a mortal sin?

The rectangular, small, slightly recessed effervescent sweets could be put into plastic hand figures whose heads spit out a sweet when folded up. There was an elk, Donald Duck, Mickey Mouse and others. I had the moose. But I always wanted to have the pi¬stole that was on the candy wrapper. On the prospectus one could see how a sweet flew out of the pi¬stole. I used to imagine owning this gun to surprise people. I never bought them.

The small official residence

Miss Vormstein had retired. She moved out of her apartment. Another place. To her sister with the pumpkins. When she moved, I thought, "This is weird. She lived here for years. Door to door with us. She worked here and went to church here. The old priest and the new priest knew their sins. Why is she leaving?

100

One day she was gone. And the apartment she lived in was empty. We had her key. Sometimes I'd go inside to play football. I shot the rubber ball full of rage in her former living room in front of the walls. This official residence had no authority anymore. Back when she housed the old, shriveled lady, every wallpaper fiber had a teacher-like power over me.

My father got sicker. He couldn't work anymore. We visited him almost daily with the car in the hospital. He had a round belly of water. His legs and feet were thick. His face is very puffy.

The family got restless. Mother always said that was from malnutrition in captivity. Although his father had recovered after the war, there were many relapses. Then my father was punctured. His stomach was back to normal size. A few weeks later, he came home. But he also lay in bed during the day and took many tablets. Mother said he was still very sick and we should pray a lot for him. So did I. Then he went to hospital again because his stomach was swelling up again. Another one this time. Further away. We went there a lot. The journey with the white Opel Kadett to Fersen to the Kreiskran-kenhaus took more than an hour.

My father was in a room on the ground floor. Single. I thought that was funny, because in the previous hospital there was another patient in the room. But he wanted a single room. That wouldn't upset him so much, he said. It was good for us, because when we visited, nobody was bothered. I often looked at the sickbed from below. The mechanics. I had something to play. My siblings came with me at irregular intervals. Saturdays and Sundays we were always together in the hospital. Then I had my toys with me. There was little time for my homework. I also couldn't concentrate on her very well.

It became apparent that my father could no longer work. He retired early. This meant giving up the official residence in the school building, because a new main teacher was to move in. In the long run we should no longer live in the old village school. Surprisingly, we moved into Fräulein Vormstein's apartment. In a short time all furniture had to be knocked off.

While my father was in hospital, the rest of the family and I were busy moving. As an alcoholic, he could neither exert himself nor get excited. Our temporary apartment was much smaller than the old one. We had to part with a lot of furniture. It was all very strange to me. For quite a while I had the hope that we would move back into our apartment, that my father would get well and be able to work.

Due to its size, my parents' wardrobe had to be set up in the bedroom so that it covered the window. There was no other place. Only the skylight remained free. So that one could ventilate, I was assigned to tinker a special construction.

With the help of a ladder I climbed the roof of the wardrobe, which was stable. With a hand drill I predrilled a hole and screwed in an eyebolt. This caused me to thread a strong band that led to the spring closure of the skylight.

Before I crawled down again, I saw our blue penalty stick hanging from the side. I was surprised, because he has always been hidden from us. Where, only my parents knew.

At first I looked at the upper floor round - it shuddered at me. I didn't know the stick was hanging here.

Because no one was watching my craft on the cupboard, I carefully took our stick into my hands for the first time and looked at it: Memories of punitive experiences. It had lost much of its original blue color and formed ugly brown patches where it had flaked off.

After a while I hung the stick back in its place.

I turned a second eyebolt into the front edge of the roof so that the threaded band could perform its deflection function. Then I got down and tried out the mechanics. It worked. You had to close the window with a long broomstick.

The key to our old apartment was temporarily kept in safe custody. There too I played football in the empty living room. I often shot the ball full of anger against the big wall where our living room cupboard with the spirits used to stand. I was a gyp. But I always had to make sure the windows weren't hit.

During a secret game in this apartment I discovered one day in the compartment of the kitchen sink left behind our enamel pot with candle wax residues in it. We'd been collecting stumps for years. The pot must have been forgotten when we moved.

I took it out and saw it was three quarters full of wax residue. Among them were wick residues, which were not sooty. When a candle has burned down, often a light piece of wick remains in the last remnant, which looks as untouched as the initial wick of an unused candle. Funny, a candle like that, I thought: it lives by giving light, but burns itself in the process. I never liked that about candles.

My brothers and sisters had sometimes poured new candles out of these wax remnants. It stank in the apartment.

Now the pot was on the shelf of the metal sink and I was looking for matches. In this apartment I found none, so I went next door and got a new parcel of world-woods.

This thick pack with the diagonally arranged match on it.

A wick looked so far out that I could light it. A small flame burned in the pot, slowly melting the surrounding wax. With time more wicks came to light. They didn't light well. Sometimes they burned briefly, but then drowned in liquid wax, extinguishing their flame.

By trial and error, I found that matches could take over the service of a wick. After I had stuck a match head up in liquid wax, I lit it. It burned from top to bottom, like a wick. At a certain point I could observe that the flame did not eat itself further, but that the wood itself became a kind of wick. It sucked the liquid wax up.

That fascinated me and I thought about putting more woods in the wax. Before I took the pot and put it in the depression of the sink. Just in case, if I had to delete it.

103

A sea of flames covered the wax. Ablace burned it in the pot and liquefied more strongly. The wax and wooden wicks now formed a common flame, which became bigger and bigger. The pot was hot, I felt that when I tried to push it aside a bit. The fire got creepy. I figured out a test to put out the flames if they burned too high.

I turned on the tap so that a sufficient amount of water flowed out. As soon as the casting reached the wax, a huge jet of flame explosively formed up to the ceiling.

I was so frightened that I jumped back and ran straight for the door to get help. Because I suspected that this meter-high flame would immediately set the room and the entire school on fire. Meanwhile, the water flowed over the wax pot. Fearfully, I regretted what I did.

When I reached the door, I heard a loud hiss in the corner. I turned around and saw a cloud of steam enveloping the dying flames.

Immediately I looked to the ceiling. She was unharmed.

Fortunately, there were no more curtains on the windows that could have given birth to the Inferno.

I breathed a sigh of relief.

Opened a window to vent the smoke. The water was in the pot and I waited until it had cooled down. The wax offered an unsightly mass. Full of bubbles and cracks.

The charred matches stood out dead.

I poured the water off after a while, pulled out the charred woods to destroy evidence, kneaded the wax a little, and put the pot back in the sink compartment.

We should move again. "Move?" I said. "Where to? Away from Kleinenbach?" "Yes," my mother said, "we're moving to Dortmund."

I completely lost my footing. At the age of twelve.

"And what about my friends - and the gymnasium?" I asked. "You'll find new friends there - and another school," she replied.

But I didn't believe her. I didn't want to move and always asked her how we couldn't stay.

"No," she said. "Your career opportunities are better in town."

I decided to write to my friends that I would leave behind.

At home we packed books and other items in boxes. Without my father. He was still in the hospital. He was supposed to come later. When everything was ready. Wallpapering, painting, carpet laying. My mother thought it was better for him. He couldn't stand the excitement, he was still very ill.

I said goodbye to Mr. Diel in grammar school. "You'll find another good school," he said.

From our new town came a big furniture truck. Four movers got out. That wasn't enough. We had to help out so it went fast enough.

In Dortmund my mother slammed the left car door of the cadet in front of my head. I wanted to get off after we got there. She'd already got out and thought I'd get out on the right.

Aunt Gertrud walked around the apartment and examined the rooms on the first floor. She was accompanied by an old woman - the landlady. The previous tenant had thrown his new coal stove from the first floor out of rage a few days earlier. Only because he couldn't use it for his new house and neither the landlord nor we wanted to buy it.

Together with my brother I had my own room. Just behind the front door on the left. There weren't any pretty skins in the street. I went to high school. The new classmates were watching me curiously. My class teacher's name was Schreiber. She was blond and very strict. We had them in German.

At some point she asked what to do about a fire that would break out at school. I was sure of the answer. Bravely and quickly I raised my arm and said: "Immediately break all the windows so that you can breathe!

"Wrong!" she said. "You have to close all the windows so there's no draught to fuel the fire."

That's how I got my first minus points from her.

Weeks after that lesson, my father was discharged from the hospital. The whiteness of his eyes was still yellowish. They said he had to keep resting and resting. In our house. Now he didn't send me to buy beer and booze anymore.

On a Friday in winter Mrs. Schreiber let us leave a little earlier. With a group of classmates I crossed the schoolyard towards the tram stop. We pushed each other, laughed loudly and looked forward to the weekend. One said there were still children upstairs in the hallway. We turned around and could see some of our classmates running around on the second floor. They grabbed their knapsacks and dressed.

I bent over and formed a snowball. Without thinking long and hard, I threw it towards the window pane and hit the pane directly opposite our class door. I hadn't planned this, but on the other hand I was proud that I had hit the target with a throw. We all looked there. Shortly afterwards Ms Schreiber appeared behind the window with some of her classmates and first looked at the snowball, which began to thaw and slowly slipped down the window pane. Then she looked at us. I had a strange feeling and wanted to hide. We turned around and went to the stop. Some children came running excitedly behind us and shouted, we should stop. We did. Uwe told us that I got a reprimand. For the snowball. The scribes would have put him down.

He saw it.

"What?" I said. "A reprimand? I don't think so. She doesn't even know I threw it. Besides, the glass isn't broken. It was all accidental. I didn't mean to hit the disc. It just happened by accident. Somebody must have ratted me out to the clerk. And she's gonna give me a reprimand! If there's three of them, they'll expel you from school. That's the first reprimand of my life. What would my parents say? They'll get a letter right away!"

They shouldn't know that at all. I feverishly thought of ways to intercept the letter. My parents had the mailbox key on their bunch of keys. He hung it from the key board in the hallway when they got home. I was uncomfortable. What was I supposed to do? A reprimand immediately. From the clerk.

I started to hate that woman. Without talking to me first, she entered a rebuke in the class register. I still didn't want to believe it.

The next Monday Mrs. Schreiber told the whole class. I became very sad and didn't know what to answer. Inside, I screamed. In my mind I resisted it with hands and feet. In thought, I replied that I thought it was unfair. Just for a little snowball that flew to the window, to give me an immediate reprimand. Even a rebuke would have been inappropriate for a quiet student like me. I imagined what my parents would say.

The blame was not only in the class register, but would also be in the testimony.

Neither Mrs. Schreiber nor her lessons I liked from now on. I once got a black travel knife as a present. That had a sharp, long, brightly flashing blade. I wanted to kill myself with this. Either cut my veins or ram it into my heart or belly.

How could I intercept the school's blue letter so it didn't fall into the hands of my parents? The mail often came after lunch. Sometimes only after my parents had taken a nap. Then I could look in the mailbox.

I did this every day, hoping that the letter would not be posted in the morning and that my parents would see it earlier than I did.

A week after my complaint, I held the letter in my hands. Although it was addressed to my father, I opened it and thus violated the secrecy of the letter. Fortunately, it was just an information letter that didn't have to be signed. But I would have done that too: forged the signature. Nevertheless, one thing was clear to me: this reprimand would definitely be in the semi-annual report, which would tell my parents about it. But not until later.

I threw the letter away.

On the day I got my report card, my stomach was swollen. How should I explain the blame to my parents? Should I be telling the truth? What would they say?

The reprimand was actually registered. It would be a tough walk for me. Shortly after I rang the bell and went up the stairs to the first floor, Marlene came up to me excitedly and said that father was in the hospital again. He'd get worse again. We'd have to get there now. My mother came and so we drove to the clinic. He lay there almost motionless and breathed heavily. The report card wasn't important anymore.

Ministrant with Uncle Eberhard

My mother said that we would go to church with her uncle, who was a pastor in the neighboring parish. We were not to go to Joseph's Church, to whose parish our residential district belonged. I didn't get that. Why didn't we go to church in our congregation? My mother said the Church was better than Joseph's Church. But I didn't believe her. And I was afraid of having to confess to my uncle. Would he tell my mother anything about my sins? Would she question him? They also met privately.

I would never confess to Uncle Eberhard that I had been outrageous. Did my father confess to him that he had committed adultery with Miss Grewen? That's a Todsün-de. Or had my father already confessed this to Reverend Seedorn? Or Reverend Nahberg? Does the same sin weigh less heavily if it is confessed more frequently to several pastors?

In my native village I had been an altar boy and had to continue my ministry in the city. Uncle Eberhard's. That's what my mother wanted.

Neighbouring children, with whom I made friends, asked whether this uncle was a brother of my mother or father.

"Neither," I said.

"Then he's not your real uncle either," the children replied.

"Yes!" I replied.

"No!" they replied.

At home, I asked my mother if Uncle Eberhard was her brother or her father's. "He's my cousin," she replied. "But you can still call him uncle because we're related." My mother only ever called him Eberhard.

It was a modern church, painted white, with a freestanding bell tower that seemed to have been sawn off at the top. I didn't like the flat roof church because it looked like a box. Our village church had a slate saddle roof, large clocks on all four sides of the integrated bell tower. And on its pyramid-shaped top a weathercock was enthroned.

When we were still living in Kleinenbach, but visited my aunt Gertrud in Dortmund, I had seen Uncle Eberhard's church for the first time. I was about eight years old and was here on holiday with my mother and Marlene.

Without my alcoholic father.

My other two siblings were in a country school home.

109

Aunt Gertrud told us about the fair that was just taking place.

We had never visited a fair before. I knew shooting parties from my village. With a shooting gallery, a chain carousel and pony rides. But a fair in town?

Aunt Gertrud asked if Marlene and I wanted to go there with her daughter Sandra after lunch. I'm sure there'd be a lot of new things for us to see. "Ouch!" I shouted, "is there a bumper car there? I want to drive a bumper car!" "But of course there are also bumper cars," Aunt Gertrud replied.

We were thrilled.

She suggested that we go on foot because we were rested and strengthened from the food. Besides, we'd save money for a tram ride.

Then we should go back by train, because running and visiting the fair would certainly make us tired.

The proposal convinced Marlene and me. Cousine Sandra got from her aunt our all fair money and additionally fare for the return journey. Our aunt forbade us to spend the fare at the fair and Sandra would show us which tram we should take.

We left my aunt's apartment building and followed the wide street over which a tram crossed. There weren't any in my village. It was ochre. An ugly ochre colour as background and Jägermeister advertising on it. The road seemed so long and my feet hurt. Besides, it was hot. The sun was shining very strongly. We were sweating.

Marlene and I were full of expectations for the fair - which drove us forward.

However, the fun was visibly spoiled by the long running. Sandra often said we should just hold out, because we'd be there soon.

The path led us past the white church and Sandra said, "This is Uncle Eberhard Pfarrer." To the right and left of the road were trees, so we had at least a bit of shade. Meanwhile we could hear music, sirens and bells. We were happy, because we came closer to the fairground. It was a huge square of red ashes. The smell of roasted almonds and cotton candy got into our noses. Motor scooters, lottery booths, Labostella, a roller coaster, a chain carousel, shooting galleries, throwing booths, a ghost train, a ferris wheel, ponies, boat swing...

Where should we go?

"For each of you I have five marks. When they're spent, we have to go home," Sandra said. "And we have to stay together so you don't get lost."

I stopped at the caterpillar first. Their wagons were driving on wooden planks in circles, mountains and valleys. When the siren sounded, a long soft top slid over the vehicles and the inmates had disappeared. Unexpectedly the tarpaulin opened again and many a boy quickly pulled away his arm, which he had on the shoulder of his companion.

We were throwing balls and riding the Ferris wheel, but the ghost train scared me. My mother had told me that there were threads hanging down there that you couldn't see because it was dark and they ran through your face. Then there would be monster-like figures and skeletons that flare up, shake and laugh gloatingly. There was no ghost train at the Rifle Festival.

A showman with a waist-high wooden box cast a spell over me: a glass pane with coloured skat motifs was embedded in the upper frame. The individual card spaces lit up irregularly when the man pressed a button. After a while the light stopped under a map. The one who bet on it was the winner. If you wanted to play, you had to put money on one or more fields. I put thirty pfennigs on seven of spades and waited eagerly to see what would happen. The light stopped at queen of haerts.

Excited, I bought chips at the cash desk and got on a bumper car with cousin Sandra. She immediately took the wheel, being the oldest at fourteen. Of course I wanted to steer, but she said I could try it later. She said she wanted to

111

drive first and I should watch. Marlene stood on the edge. A siren sounded, the lights on the scooters lit up and we were off. The steel field was bigger than what I knew from Kleinenbach. There were more cars, too.

Sandra carefully steered the car along the gang and avoided bumping into others. I couldn't wait to drive the car. After Sandra's second trip we changed places. She had to insert the chip so that I - with both hands on the handlebars - could drive off immediately. With my ass I slipped to the edge of the bench to get my foot to the gas pedal. Now I remembered the assemblers at the shooting match. It honked. Slowly I stepped down the pedal and felt the power of the engine. I already had to avoid an oncoming car, otherwise we would have collided. We went around to the left. Like most of them. I didn't dare go backwards. It was too restless here for that. But I still enjoyed it. After the trip Sandra and Marlene exchanged, so that she also sat once in the scooter. When the power was switched off again, all chips were used up and Sandra wanted to go on with us.

Bull horns, snack stands, love thermometers.

Two muscular men stood in front of a device with a large dial carrying words and laughed loudly. The ad jumped up into the vertical when he inserted a coin in his red T-shirt. Then he pulled out and hit the thick leather pad with his right fist. The pointer stopped at Mother's boy. Now only the one who hadn't played laughed. Those who had more strength could become astronauts, boxers, heroes, show-offs or good lovers.

From the remaining money I bought two wonder bags, a water pistol with rotating muzzle and liquorice. Then it was time to leave. Sandra said we could also walk back. First of all it would not be far, because we knew the way now and secondly we would save money. Sandra was one year older than Marlene and thus the oldest. She lived in this town, knew her way around and supervised us. If Marlene and I

112

were to resist, she would certainly squeal on my aunt later and say that we were squeamish and naughty.

Marlene and I didn't dare contradict Sandra. For a moment I thought Sandra was right - the way was really not far - but when we had walked a few meters I regretted the thought. We nagged. Sandra just said we'd be right there. So we slouched back this long way and passed the white church again.

Exhausted, we arrived at my aunt's. The pleasure and fun of the fair had passed us by. "Wasn't it beautiful?" my aunt asked enthusiastically.

Out of sheer courtesy, my sister and I answered yes.

Uncle Eberhard was a small man around fifty, with corners of his mouth pulled down and a creeping gait. This passage, which a priest has, who leaves the sacristy with humility before God during the organ playing at the beginning of Mass. In the hand the chalice with the square cardboard lid. Over it the linen cloth with the red embroidered cross on it. This priest looked at the concealed chalice every time he went in and out. I was therefore surprised that he did not cause any altar boys to stumble, for he did not see their feet. The ministrant lessons took place on Thursday afternoon in an adjoining room of the community office. Fifteen altar boys sat there during my first visit. But there was more in the community.

Among them were students from my class that I met here again. Uncle Eberhard asked why so few altar boys had come today. At first, no one wanted to answer. But in response to the repeated question Dieter said that the series Fantomas was shown on television. It was more exciting and his friends didn't want to miss it.

Uncle Eberhard folded his forehead and replied disappointedly: "Obviously television is more important to some than God".

I was surprised that Horst, Klaus, Albert, Frank and Georg were absent from this important lesson just because a series was on television. My classmates were more religious and I had never had the courage not to appear on Thursday afternoon.

I didn't know that from the village. All the altar boys were present. Unless someone's been sick. Like my brother.

First Uncle Eberhard set the weekly schedule. Who would serve when? There were morning masses, the least liked, because you had to get up early. Evening fairs, Sunday and holiday fairs. Then devotions, funeral masses and weddings. Older altar boys were sometimes allowed to choose dates. There were also volunteers who volunteered several times because they enjoyed serving.

They named their desired fair and were registered.

I was new to the parish and first had to get to know the church, the uncle as a pastor and the municipal ministrant service. Consequently, I was assigned to the experienced.

After the plan was discussed, my uncle took a book out of his briefcase and read it out. Just as hard as he preached the sermon. Dry, without noticeable movement. In the book there was the word Filou. Some boy was a filou. Uncle Eberhard asked us if anyone knew the word. No one could explain it. That's what he did. When trouble arose, he handed the book around. The one who wanted to read should read. Hopefully I wouldn't get to it, I thought. I hated public reading. When class was over, a bright summer sunbeam hit me. I went home by bike.

Sometimes I visited friends from my class by bike. Some played soccer. Some of them were in a swimming club. Others went to piano lessons or learned to play the recorder. My father, who had been discharged from the hospital, sat with me on some afternoons and played something on the piano for me to practice. Strictly by grades: Summ, Summ, Summ, Bienchen, hum around.

114

But the hours with him were no fun for me, because my parents wanted to make a famous pianist out of me and exerted strong pressure. Their prestige thinking scared me and so I soon gave up.

Most of the time, however, my father would lie on the couch when I got out of school. And resting. He read in the daily newspaper, in the mirror or listened to music with a medium wave radio. My father and his little battery-powered medium-wave radios. In the toilet, in the woods or just before bed: Radio, radio, radio.

When his health was better, my mother considered whether he wanted to play the organ in Uncle Eberhard's church. You could initiate the conversation. "It would be nice if he would play there," she said to us. There wouldn't be any good organisations at the moment. And he should slowly try again. Besides, he'd have another job to do.

At some point you could hear my father playing the organ in this church. At first only on Sundays. However, there was no pipe organ here, as in our old village church, but an electronic organ whose sound could be strongly distinguished from that of a classical organ. My father said at the time that he didn't want to play it because it worked electronically. But my mother replied that the church was collecting for a pipe organ. That would take a few years, but the congregation would like a pipe organ.

Organ players have it good. They can influence church events with their play and do not need to sit down. You're sitting on a hill. Yes, they always sit over the heads of the faithful and that of the priest and the altar boys. They form an authoritarian counterweight to the priest.

Not just from her art of playing.

Also by the spatial division: the priest is always well visible, at the brightly illuminated altar in his church uniform. The altar boys and faithful look at him and want to be guided through the liturgy. He radiates a powerful clerical power at the push of a button and is confident during the performance of his role. The organist, on the other hand, is in civil and does not have the competence of a priest because of this appearance.

My father sneaked out of the sacristy shortly before the event, after consultation with the pastor. Past the coughing and murmuring praying audience. In a humiliated attitude, he went to the organ loft. He was hardly noticed. He might as well have been one of the viewers. Only when the song number was thrown against the wall with the projector and the music sounded did everyone know that he was there.

However, he was able to strike the keys with a mighty punch and, by registering the organ accordingly, show the cleric where the notes hang.

I believe that my father often wanted to suggest to Uncle Eberhard what he thought of him. Because both fought not only in the sacristy, but also privately.

The question is whether unmusical people like this priest understand such organ signals. Or didn't he want to understand her?

Sometimes I took part in services as an altar boy. I also had to wear a robe. In one part of the sacristy there was a separate dressing room for altar boys. A room with a full-length closet, where all the uniforms were hung. At normal masses, the black and white altar boy's robe was quickly put on and the priest waited until he had finished dressing and had left the sacristy. The group quickly formed up and opened the door to the church room. The hands were folded and we left the room with a creeping gait.

The small signal bell was activated.

From that moment on, believers and organists knew that the spiritual train was in motion.

After three steps, it went around to the right. Past the first rows of banks. Mothers who had their sons turned into altar boys were certainly proud of them at that moment. I felt uncomfortable in the altar boy's robe, for my feeling said that my mother wanted a altar boy for pure prestige reasons.

I felt constantly watched - as in school lessons - and was glad not to have to take on any special tasks, such as reading the Holy Scriptures. That's how I did my duty. Kneeled at the altar. I took the handbell and tinkling.

I wasn't allowed to operate the incense burner. Not even now, at the age of fifteen.

Only older altar boys were allowed to do that because of the embers in the vessel. However, I once had the chance to refill incense granulate during the fair, because an altar boy was ill at short notice, who should have done it.

The priest was brought chalice, bread, water and wine. Held the cloth to dry his fingers. Sometimes I thought that was superfluous. Because he often didn't have wet hands. Yet he wiped it off.

The sermon was delivered while three other altar boys and I sat on the right side of the altar archor. I didn't understand much about what Uncle Eberhard said about the pulpit. I was dim. But I had to be attentive, because the audience always looked towards the Altarchor and registered every movement there - even if the attention was mainly directed to Uncle Eberhard.

Surprisingly, a fart came loose, which was unmistakable. I looked stubbornly straight ahead, but at the same time I felt that my face was getting very hot. Nevertheless I looked further forward, listened to the sermon and tried, as the chairs did not give way, to make a similar noise to the farting noise of my leather shoes afterwards, in order to convince my altar boy colleagues that the fart did not come from inside.

But they weren't stupid and noticed my diversion because they looked over at me. The heat slowly disappeared from my face.

I was embarrassed.

Did my uncle hear anything?

And the believers?

Was that a sin? Could Uncle Eberhard have heard it in the pulpit at all?

Or did he hear it but not let on?

Of course, my comrades would address me squeaking in the sacristy. And maybe Uncle Eberhard too! So until then I had to think of a plausible explanation.

Lying or telling the truth?

Christian Bedor is a book author, postcard artist, Müllzeit-Los-Croupier and cabaret artist. M.A., Film Studies, Modern Philology, Media Sociology. Christian Bedor already wrote franked letters to his classmates during his regular school days. This was followed by poems, short stories, satirical fragments for the cabaret stage as well as photo and text contributions for the Mail Art projects UNI/VERS(;) (ed.: Guillermo Deisler, Halle/Saale) and DIE SPINNE (ed.: Dirk Fröhlich; Dresden). Special thanks go to Joseph W. Huber, Edition Karte'll, Berlin. At the end of the 1980s he created photo and text motifs for b/w postcards. Later followed colour postcards on wit, satire and aesthetics, which have been on sale since 1996. At the same time Christian Bedor developed the mobile entertainment raffle Müll-Zeit-Lose plus exhibition stand. In recent years, countless people have drawn lots at his red vendor's trash can and won his art products: movies, books, postcards. Since several years ALEX-TV, Berlin, broadcasts monthly the satirical film series Personalberatung Team Verreckt, PTV, - Arbeitskabarett - in which Bedors garbage cans play a central role. PTV-film sequences can be found on Mediathek-Hessen (link see below). PTV-Clips on various video portals on the Internet.

Publications

Beichtgang
Fiktive Autobiografie eines katholischen Hauptlehrersohns
Print book/eBook, audio book CD - read by author
Kreatives Marketing für Künstler
Print-Book/eBook - 366 daily texts with index
Bewegungsversuche
Print-Book/eBook - stories by Christian Bedor and
Michael Liebusch
Das Diapendel
Print-Book/eBook - novel
Kussweilig Print-Book/eBook
dream letters, aphorisms, poems
Schrittweiß
Print-Book/eBook - story

Personalberatung Team Verreckt – Cabaret-Series
87 DVD movies

26 different **postcards**-(motifs) from the
areas of wit, satire and aesthetics

BoD-Buchshop:
https://www.bod.de/buchshop/catalogsearch/result/index/?q=Christian+Bedor&cont_id=5073

Website of the artist: https://www.muell-zeit-lose.de

Mediathek-Hessen Vids Personalberatung Team Verreckt:
https://www.mediathek-hessen.de/index.php?ka=1&ska=suche&suchwort=Christian+Bedor

Amazon author page:
https://www.amazon.de/Christian-Bedor/e/B005BXY0AC